# PARTIAL ABSOLUTION

# PARTIAL ABSOLUTION

An exile returns to the neighborhood

By

# Ken Ross

More Ken Ross Novels:

The Lads Will Have Blood (Crime Thriller)
A Cross of Crocuses (Family Saga)
ANN: irresistible spirit (Romance)
The Ken Ross Romantic/Erotic Suspense Series:
   Wasted Pain
   Protection
   Bodies
   Mama
   Broken Sisters
   Goodbye Violet
An Old Affair (Romance)
Louann's Home Movie (Erotic Suspense)
Rosalee's Punishment (Erotic Suspense)
The Last Days of Childhood (Young Adult)
Wrapped in Green Comfort (Literary Fiction)
Rosa's Confessions/Erotic Suspense Series:
   Superfluous
   Partial Absolution

# PARTIAL ABSOLUTION

## Happy Birthday to Rosa, Happy Birthday to me

Every girl expects a birthday to be special but there is nothing special about gazing across the gray English Channel on a cold spring day with limited funds and early holidaymakers walking by with smiling faces.  I decided yesterday… exile ends today.  This lonesome chick is returning to face the music, and if necessary, visit my parents' house with a hoover stuck up her ass, never mind a sweeping brush.  I've had my fill of talking to myself or the seagulls, and a girl of twenty-six shouldn't be building sand-castles all day.

I board a train in Brighton and spend over six hours (including changes of the train) to get to my hometown of Leeds.  Happy homecoming!  The platform isn't filled with well-wishers even though I've not touched local menfolk in over seven long months.  Daringly, I come out of the railway station and shout quite loudly, 'Rosa Saint John is back'.  Two young lads look at me, nudge each other, then one steps in front of me and asks for an autograph.  He must think I'm famous.  I feel like asking him if I can share his bedroom – I've no place else to go.

I sniff the air, daftly rejoice that my lungs will be once more polluted and walk between two taxis to the other side of the road.  It's good to hear local accents, good to know that nobody's going to say, 'You're from up North'.  Up here we don't confront folks to tell them that they're from 'down South'.  Strange world, but I'm back to normality, among those who call a spade a spade and a girl who sleeps around a tart or a whore.

To get used to being back in Leeds, and because I've become a scrooge through my impecuniosity, I decide to walk the 3.odd miles to the east of the city. Three or four pounds will buy me a meal so why spend it on bus fare – I don't know where my next penny is coming from. Add to this, I don't know where my next sleep is going to be, and I don't know which familiar voice I'm going to hear first. Maybe a charity worker will somehow guess my predicament and say, 'Hey, girl, are you homeless? Tonight, half of my bed is empty. You're in luck.'

The 166 bus to Castleford passes me and I wave to the fortunate who can pay to be transported to Selby Road. The passengers on state benefits look down on me – they have homes to go to and payments to receive next Tuesday. Do I sound like a girl who feels sorry for herself?

Well, I'm not.

After seven months flitting from town to town, switching jobs every three and a half minutes, begging old people to spare a pound for a cup of coffee, finding only three young guys willing to have sex with me for the price of a burger and chips, I'm not down in the mouth or without hope of a brighter future. I'm not the Old Rosa who'd be afraid to offend anyone who didn't know me, I'm more forthright, and if I've to be a bit bold to get my feet under someone's table, then I shall be bold – only the strong survive; the weak end up burying their heads in Caroline's bush, but I'll get around to Caroline if and when she comes up.

I walk on, reach York Road, I am thankful my bag is light and not cumbersome. After a mile or two I begin to wonder if I'll be recognized – 'There goes the girl who starred in 'Orgy In The Golf Club'', 'There goes the only girl who could keep pace with Tracey Cummings', or even, 'There goes 'Rosa Saint John who used to be a nice girl'. Buses don't screech to a halt, and neither do cars.  The daylight is fading and I'm already wondering if I'll be cuddling up to a tree in the churchyard with a hunky ghost for company.


**Strange Meeting**

I'm sure it was Wilfred Owen's soldier in his famous poem that talked to a ghost.  If I don't get a move on the living will have gone to bed and only ghosts will be up and active.  I pass what used to be the Shaftesbury Cinema and see all the familiar buildings in the foreground and to the horizon.  Here I go again, I start talking to myself, 'Rosa, you are home.  Rosa go to your house, open the door and surprise Marty.  Tell him you don't mind sharing a pillow with Caroline providing that's where she puts her head and not her hairy crotch.'

Marty, my ex, hasn't heard from me since last August.  He likely thinks I'm propping up lampposts in the red light district on the other side of town.  That's supposing he thinks of me because by now he'll be on fifteen little blue pills a day and permanently fixated with the problem of carrying his manhood around in an extra-long shopping trolley.  Stuff Marty – my old house is the last port of call on my list; my problem is that I don't possess a list.

In another fifteen minutes, I'm wandering about my former haunts and gluing my eyes on anyone I see on the streets. Do folks age in seven months?  Guys grow beards, girls let themselves go, kids shoot up like ignited rockets and others die or move away just like I did.  Don't pass me by, say if you think I look like Rosa Saint John.  I'll flash my bits to prove that I am her.

A familiar voice resonates from the doorway of the local store that banned me because I returned a moldy loaf, 'Is that you?  Hell, it is you!' yells Belinda.  She comes up to me pushes my shoulder, 'Have you gone back to him?'

'Who?'

'Marty, of course.'

'I've just returned today... now, I'm looking for somewhere to rest my feet.'

Belinda folds her arms even though she's bags attached to both.  That's a sign for NO ENTRY.  'You know what my bloke is like.  He won't let the kids' mates in the house, let alone...'

'A tart?' I say.

She wafts her bags.  'Nice to have seen you, Rosa... you take care now and let me know how you go on.'

At least I've proved to myself that memories from last year don't vanish.  I guess I used to look so stunning in my see-through skirt and top that I'm classified as unforgettable.  Some women don't trust such a girl in the company of their husbands.

The moon shines brighter as it gets darker though clouds are amassing in the east, the temperature falls, my breath forms mists in front of my face and the tips of my fingers tingle.  I'd planned for a tough home-coming but it's a good five degrees colder than on the South Coast and no-one around is selling hot cups of coffee to warm my hands on.

My phone rings.  Yippee – the charity workers have heard my cries!  They haven't... it's my sister Katy who disowned me eight months ago, maybe nine months ago.  'Happy birthday,' she says coldly.

I make my voice tremble as though I'm seconds from dying of hyperthermia.  'Th..th...thanks, K...K...Katy.'

'Where are you?' she snaps.

'Just g...g...got off the train – I'm back in Leeds.'

'Back where?'

'Back nowhere... I've n...n...nowhere to go.'

'Oh.' There's a long pause. 'I'll call you tomorrow.' She
ends the call. She'll take time to bury the hatchet, that's if she
ever finds a place to put it.

Well, it's an achievement I guess – on earth for twenty-six
years and one person wishes me happy birthday. I'm ahead of
hermits and monks who live in silence. I'm on the way up.

And just as I think that I'm on the way up, the skies begin
depositing rain-bombs on my head; half-way across the field that
leads to the council estate I don't know where to run for shelter.
There is a small wood to the left and a road runs on the bottom
edge of the field. My heart tells me to sprint to Tracey Cumming's
house but I can't face being rejected a second time because she
loved me too much. I dart to the bus shelter on the road, arrive
there soaked to the skin, shivering, and think I'd be as well in the
sea at Brighton. Happy birthday – it's a blessing I've not got a
cake with 26 burning candles. Maybe folk who leave Leeds once
should never return.


**The drenched, the bad, and the ugly**

When I was a little girl father used to say that men without wives
are dangerous animals. Even today, or at least up to my leaving,
father still comes out with crazy statements. I don't miss him one
jot but I think of him as I wait for a dangerous animal to come
along.

Otters, sharks, polar bears pass but no young men looking
for a wet slapper. I'm doomed to wait in the bus shelter until the
next boat arrives. I eat a banana from my luggage, lighten the
burden of weight but not the burden of woe. The rain looks in for

the night.  I imagine that the next living thing I see will be a humpback whale.

Eventually, I see the silhouette of an elderly man coming toward the shelter; the man is trying to run but only his arms are sprinting.  He ducks inside, shakes his head like a wet dog and expels a sound that's similar to one from a prolonged fart.  He curses many times, then when he finishes cursing, he looks at me and informs me that no buses come here at this time of night because kids with bricks vandalize them.  The streetlamp must be illuminating my face; he tilts his head, takes a step closer.  'Aren't you that pal of Tracey Cummings who went missing a year ago?' he says.

'I'm back,' I say.  Slowly the penny drops – I assumed the guy was close to eighty but it's Kev and Timmy's father; he's surely in his sixties and the three of them live in the cul-de-sac across the field.  I know, being doubly screwed by his sons was my first boy/boy on girl sex act as my relationship with Marty was crumbling.  They tossed me into their garden naked – I walked home without knickers and with their leftovers trickling down my thighs.

He notices I'm saturated, tells me I should get home and change.  I laugh, 'What home?'  Do I plead desperately and seek refuge?  He mentions that his name is Geoff, then says somewhat kindly that his radiators are hot, and if I need to dry my clothes, they're available.  I don't hesitate, and as if by some miracle the torrential rain turns to light rain.  He suggests we make a run to his house.  I just know that his sons will be ready to put a cloth bag over my head and carry me upstairs to a bedroom, just like last time when Geoff sat in the backroom and listened to my screams.

I don't care, I'll be warm and dry.  Nothing in life comes free.  Two minutes later we're are rushing through his hallway and to the furthest doorway.  I shiver, look in my bag as I drop it on the floor and see I've been transporting a pool and my spare clothes are also soaked.  Geoff points to the radiators as he takes off his coat and hangs it over the back of the sofa; he's relatively dry and sits in his armchair and stares at me.

There is no sign of Kev and Timmy.  Geoff doesn't offer a towel but keeps nodding at the radiators.  Shame went months ago, I take off my jacket, top, and skirt and hang them on a long radiator.  Geoff ogles my body, says, 'You're a pretty girl.'  I stand not knowing what to do.  He digs in his pocket, takes out a fiver, holds it out like it's a million-dollar bill.  'How about sitting on my knee?'

I slap my ass and raindrops fly from my knickers.  'Like this,' I say.

He swaps the fiver for a tenner.  I'm no prostitute but I do need money.  'Twenty,' I say.  Geoff offers two notes.  I don't think, remove my wet underwear, add it to the radiator, then go sit sideways on his lap.  He keeps his hands away from my body but his eyes are transfixed; they roam up and down and he keeps telling me that I'm fabulous.

I'm patient, happy to be drying and happy to be warm.  It takes him ten minutes before he asks if he can touch my tits.  I nod.  He's gentle and almost fearful of being slapped in the face. He compliments me and in a roundabout way says he's sorry that he can't perform like his sons.  He's been impotent for years and he's forgotten what it's like to feel a woman.  A girl like me should never be without a place to rest her head.  And this goes on and I get to wonder if I could make a living sitting on old men's knees.

A year ago, I wouldn't have done this for a fortune, but now it's so easy, and if he were capable, I wouldn't mind doing more.

Geoff eventually goes silent; he stares contently at my tits. I hear footsteps on the stairs then Kev and Timmy barge through the door wearing only their boxers. They gawp when they see me. 'Fucking hell, she's back,' says Timmy the youngest.

'Wake up, give her one,' says Kev to his father. They go to the kitchen, get cans of beer and for a few seconds, I'm convinced I'll be dragged up the stairs and screwed without mercy. Instead, they return to the upper floor and I'm left somewhat amazed, and maybe a little disappointed. Geoff stirs.

'What's wrong with them?' I say.

'They've both got girlfriends in their beds, they won't touch you,' he says.


**Things can only get better**


I sneak out of Geoff's house with all my clothes dry at 7.30 in the morning. Funnily enough, I recalled all the times when Marty promised me sex then later proffered the excuse that he felt tired. From the moment I recognized Geoff, my insides were preparing for a hammering and the only thing I dreaded was being tossed naked into the garden in the dead of night. I feel let down and it's brought old physical desires racing through parts where they used to race unceasingly. I don't know who'll want me, but I'd give my hard-earned twenty to have sex with just about anyone who comes along. Maybe for a girl like me, it's impossible to make a living from sitting on old men's knees.

I skirt the field because it's muddy, then go up the side of the church to the lane that runs along its rear. When I reach the road, I dawdle by the curb knowing it's about the time when Marty passes in his car on his way to the office.  Will he pull up if he sees me?  It's worth a shot at finding out.

My phone rings, 'Be here for ten.  Brian's at work, the kids are at school,' says Katy.  At least there's one person who still loves me.


**I do the unthinkable**

Bad blood has been spilled.  Katy despised what I became and to my family members, it came as a relief when I disappeared.  Who wants a whore as a sister, aunty, or daughter?  Who needs locals thinking that the Saint John's clan descends from a tribe of Jezebels?  It's going to be awkward when we meet face to face.  My sister is prim and proper; she thinks sex is solely for making babies.  My one consolation is that she loves me.  She loves me, yet she never shows it explicitly.

When I get to her house she's standing watching from the window.  Katy is a nice-looking girl with long brown hair parted in the center.  She has those creases arcing down from her nose, just like father.  She's tall, slim, sexy for a twenty-nine-year-old and has no idea that many men other than Brian would love to take her to bed.  I wave.  She doesn't smile, merely comes to the door and stands aside as I enter.

'Where did you sleep,' she says immediately.

'In a bus shelter,' I say.

'You smell fusty.'

'Nothing I've done,' I say in code for I haven't just had sex.

She looks me up and down, opines that I've lost a pound or two in weight, then bows her head and stares from the top of her eyeballs as if to ask if I've reformed my habits. I wear a little girl expression that pleads with her not to be judgmental and at the same time begs for her pity. God, I'm thrilled to bits when she puts her hands at the side of my elbows and tells me to go get in the shower. That's the most love I've felt since my last session with Tracey Cummings.

I dump my bag in the hall, purposely put my phone on the top of the bag and then run up the stairs. I turn right to the bathroom, quickly strip, quicker still get the water running then creep back to the small landing and listen. Sure enough, she's inspecting my phone, probably viewing the call register to see if I've been in touch with Tracey or have a long, long list of men's phone numbers. I don't, and I haven't spoken to Tracey since I left last year. It's victory; my sister will look on me as a repentant woman.

I swathe my body with soap and make a thousand wishes for sex in the coming days. I fantasize that Katy has a nice young man lined up for me; she's going to convert me to a proselyte of the missionary-position and get me married off before my twenty-seventh birthday. Before thirty I'll have two snotty daughters called Penelope and Hyacinth and perhaps a poodle dog named Leslie. I'll take the nice young man and screw him senseless; she can keep the follow-ups.

But what happens next is more shocking than Geoff staring at an erection. I can normally predict things; oh yes, I was wrong about the brothers at Geoff's, but they'd acquired girlfriends and probably emptied their barrels. This time predictions went down the shower drain.

The bathroom door opens.  Katy whispers, 'You okay, Rosa?'

'Come in,' I say.

She's holding two fluffy towels.  I leave the shower and stand close to her.  She hands me the towels.  We look into each other's eyes.  I know she's wanting to ask me about the secret I have kept about her husband, Brian.  I could have blown their marriage to smithereens last summer, but I didn't.  What she's thinking is different to me.  I must admit, to be within touching distance of the one person in the world who loves me, stark naked, with a body glowing from hot water, is something of a turn on.  It's my sister.  I see her eyes fall; I know she's not got the guts to ask.  Without considering anything, I step forward, press my whole body against Katy's then lift her head and kiss her.  This is no ordinary kiss, this is a kiss that says if she's willing I'll push her across the landing to her bedroom, I'll show her what it feels like to have real sex, I'll show how powerful my attraction was to Tracey Cumming's body, I'll leave her breathless, fulfilled, take her to heaven several times if she wants me to.  The kiss lasts a minute.  I can tell she's weakening.  I press my hips harder.  Katy, submit!  Katy, submit!  When the unthinkable happens, don't pass it by.

She shudders.  'Happy birthday for yesterday,' she says like it's the reason she's allowed our lips to touch and remain touched.

'I'm always here for you,' I say which again is code for 'you know how I could change your way of life'.  She backs away, tells me that we're going to see one of her neighbors, of course when I'm dressed.  She glances at my body and I feel I've left an impression.  I shuffle my feet to tell her it's hers, take it, girl.  But

Katy retreats downstairs.  What a game-changer – my sister has inspected my curves!


**Trailer for sale or rent**

A few doors up from Katy's I meet Harry and Sally; they don't look old enough to have left school, let alone be house owners.  There is a caravan in their front garden and Katy has arranged a viewing.  As I'm uncertain of what's going on, I go with the flow, allow Katy to lead the conversation while I eye up potential bed-partners.  Harry's no more than 66 inches yet he's immensely handsome, and Sally looks so innocent that she doesn't read why I'm drooling at the mouth; she likely thinks I have a problem with my glands.

The three of them chat but I don't listen.  The shower incident has me dwelling on sex.  From Katy to Harry to Sally and around in circles I'm working myself into a sweat.  I haven't been like this for months and months and I'm yet to see Marty or Tracey Cummings.

I'm staring at Katy's tiny breasts when suddenly Katy grabs my hand and plonks a key in the center of my palm.  I thank her, though why, I don't know.  I'm led from the house, chastised for not being talkative.  'I was thinking of you,' I tell Katy and she appears a tad embarrassed though she knew perfectly what I meant.

She makes me a coffee.  I can't keep my eyes off her ass.  Then she gets serious, sits on a stool and puts her hand on the outside of my leg.  'So, it's clear, I hope.  No going out when Brian is home and may see you.  No going out when the girls are going to and from school.  You must come and go via the top of the street.  No passing my house.  No staring from the window.  And no overnight guests.'

'What?' I say.

'The caravan.  It will stay in Sally's garden and I'll pay the fifty pounds a week rent until you get on your feet.  But you must never, ever let Brian see you there.'

I bend forward like I'm going to repeat the kiss in the bathroom.  Katy offers me her cheek.  'Let's get you settled,' she says.  She gives me a hundred pounds in cash.  I collect my bag and phone, then off we go to get comfortable in my new temporary home.


**Something is happening**


Mid-afternoon in the caravan.  I have the blinds down.  I'm lying on the sofa that loops around one end, in a bathrobe my sister has given me, naked beneath, letting all the thoughts I used to have about sex rise from my memory.  Odd, how I spent all those months away and thought more about food, shelter and survival. The familiar Leeds air and the knowledge that I'm among folks I know must have changed my outlook.  I long to be screwed, long for the warmth and softness of skin.  I start thinking about Tracey Cummings and before I realize what I'm doing the ends of the bathrobe belt are in my hands.  I imagine her bound on her dirty pink bedsheet and she's begging me to hurt her and calling me a bitch because I'm showing patience.  My toes sense the flattened carpet that surrounds her bed.  I zoom in on her body and see her paperwhite thighs twitching, anticipating my moves, reacting already to what has not yet been done.  I lick my lips, lick my lips as a hand taps on the caravan door and in walks Katy.  One flap of the bathrobe falls on the side of the sofa.  Katy takes a pace or two closer, says softly, 'You prefer being naked, don't you?'  She smiles, tries to hide what she feels by referring to me as a young child who loved to run about without clothes.

'And you,' I said.

'Me,' murmured Katy.

'What do you...' I alter the question.  'How do you prefer me?'

Oh God, the most erotic few seconds of the past months electrify both of us.  I touch myself and Katy watches me.  I'm reeling her in, see submission wash over her face, and I beckon her to get nearer still.  It looks like she's in a dream.  I will her to kneel and she does kneel.  I will her to place her hand on my skin and she touches my belly.  My fingers rake her silky hair and I force her head toward mine.  I kiss her as I kissed her in the bathroom and she is responsive, opening her mouth and letting our tongues meet.  When I release her, I tell her I want her, want her now.  I feel her breasts, catch her hand as it withdraws and attempt to steer it back to my skin.

'This is so wrong,' says Katy.

'People all over the world sin,' I say.

'Not like this.'

'You're the only person in the world who loves me.'

I try to take her in my arms but she resists.  She tells me that I'm beautiful.  She can see what men see in me.  I've caused her to question her beliefs in the hours since this morning.  'My mind is in turmoil,' she says.

'Katy... I want you,' I say.

She looks terrified, half blows me a kiss before walking back to the door and leaving.

**An attempt at daughterhood**

I've grown used to my own company.  The night was long but not wasted in the comfort of the caravan.  After I'd watched for Brian going to work, then waited for Katy to return after taking her daughters to school, I called to see her.

She busied herself from the first moment; she dreaded our eyes meeting, dreaded more another kiss for she desired to go to bed with me and taste something of the adventures I tasted after Marty cheated on me.  What's more, she knew that secret in my keeping would drive her into my arms.  She had her home and her daughters to consider.  Please don't force me, Rosa.  Please tell me why you have called then rid me of this temptation.

'I wish I were as gorgeous as you,' I said.

She purposely wiped a dirty cloth on her face.  I tell her that I'm going to call on our parents.  I won't mention where I'm staying.  I won't say that we are… getting on, or anything.  Katy wishes me luck but dare not watch me leave.

As I walk the half-mile or so to my parents my desires ease a little although I do mull over possibilities of searching for Marty (likely at work) and Tracey (likely out on the pull).  From the outside my parents' house and garden look tidier; there is a small bed of flowers in the middle of the lawn and a new wooden railing at the side of the path.  I'm philosophical – a bucket of shit thrown at my face wouldn't be a surprise.  I tap on the door and enter.  Father sees me first and cries, 'Look what the wind's blown in!'

Mother rushes from the kitchen.  'You've got a cheek,' she says nastily.

'A cheek for what?'

'I hope nobody saw you.  Folks have long memories. You're a disgrace to the family,' she snarls.

Father wafts his hand, telling me not to respond to mother.  Mother barges past me and heads to the staircase.  I step into the room and father listens and waits for her to climb the stairs.  I notice they've been spending – lots of their rubbish has gone and they now own a large television on a posh stand.

'She hasn't forgiven you, Rosa.  That film of you at the Golf Club left her traumatized.  A woman feels helpless when she's watching her daughter be violated.  I know you went there voluntarily, but all those folks watching you...'

'And what did you think?' I say.

He grins, looks to the television like he's had a few viewings.  'I'm surprised that you're not famous by now.'

'How are you both?'

'Not bad, love,' he says.

He tells me to get a cup of tea.  I make an excuse.  I get a strong urge to leave.  After another minute of awkward conversation, I kiss him on top of the head and depart.  It's hard to believe that not long ago I scrubbed their house three or four times a week.  They are strangers to me.  Shall I ever return?

I wander to the shopping precinct to see the café where I used to work with Josivini before I lost my job and she went back to Fiji to see her folks.  The shutters are down; a notice fixed to the brickwork reads UNIT TO LET.  Those days are gone, just like my days on the South Coast.  Then I'm drawn in the direction of my former home and as I pass through the streets wonder if Marty still thinks of me – is he happily settled with Caroline, even moved to her place and sold our 'love nest'.

It takes courage to face failed relationships.  From a hundred yards off I see no sign of Marty's car.  I hurry along the pavement then at the last second, just before passing the house, I dart across the tarmac and peep through the front window.  Rapid sweeps of the eye tell me little has changed.  He must still be there; my ornaments are in place, my mirrors, souvenirs I bought on holiday and nothing to suggest black-bush Caroline has taken over.  I skip a couple of steps to the pavement and feel vaguely triumphant as I take the first left and out of sight of former neighbors.  Bravery reaps dividends.  I don't love Marty but I wouldn't refuse an offer to move back home.

Not content, I ride my luck.  I head along the road that leads to the bus shelter where I encountered Geoff.  I start stringing sentences that I'm going to say to Tracy Cummings – sure love is painful Tracey; you gave me up because you couldn't stand the pain; you gave me up solely for sex when you could have had both.  What's it like now – haven't you yearned for my body as I've yearned for yours?  For God's sake, if you still love me, let's get it on.  You and me, forever, like it used to be.

In five minutes, I'm turning her front door handle.  The door is locked.  I call as loud as I dare through the letterbox, only the tick of a clock.  'Bitch', I say.  Is she hiding or screwing in a foreign bed?  Luck never lasts for long.  Now I feel deflated.


**A taste of honey**

I see Katy once in the afternoon; she looks scared of me, or more accurately scared of being manipulated.  I have her running from her feelings; those kisses made her tingle and I know that by the way she looked at my body she hit a wall of attraction.  If one sister can have lesbian tendencies then so can the other even if she has a shit of a husband and two snotty daughters.  What goes on in a woman's body stays there – a new kind of thirst needs quenching.  Sooner or later I'm going to be irresistible and Katy's going to spend the rest of her life torn between women and men, just as I am, or just as I've been in the recent past.

I go to my new 'luxury accommodation' before Katy leaves for school. I eat a few snacks, lock the door, strip down to my underwear and turn up the heating. What's an aching girl got to do for the next sixteen hours but amuse herself?

And the hours drip past. I muse over relationships, list all those who I've been with, list those who I'd dally with, list those who I desire. It's not going to work out ideally, I know. Life isn't perfect. Ideals are gobbled up by opportunity. What's expedient often supersedes that which is most desired. I desire my sister, desire Tracey Cummings, but no doubt I'll end up next to Marty in our stained bed or spending hours every evening on old Geoff's lap. Let's hope Kev and Timmy dump their girlfriends and they use their unspent energy on me.

Time goes snail-pace to eight in the evening; all I've heard is a few passing cars and Harry go out on his motorbike. I've not been idle, but the details are personal. Then I think I hear a noise that's coming from my landlady's side door.

Peeping between slats in the blind I see a middle-aged man counting money into Sally's hand – doing business on a doorstep is hardly customary, but hey, she's a young girl alone in a big house. The guy has a clipboard. When he finishes counting money, he hands the clipboard to Sally, gives her a pen and instructs her to sign on a dotted line. He gets her to sign a sheet under the top sheet. Soon after, he bids her goodnight, then passes the caravan and leaves. She'd already shut her door and I think that's it. Nothing to do with me, but I keep watching.

A gust blows. I see a banknote somersault close to her door. I could use the money but at the same time think I could maybe endear myself to Sally by being honest. Still in my underwear and unconcerned what Sally will think of me, I unlock my door, saunter to the side of the house and pick up the banknote. She has a doorbell, I press it, acquire a kind smile and wait.

Sally opens the door. She's stunned because I'm half-naked. 'Looking for fun?' I joke as I pass her the banknote. She's bemused now. 'You must have dropped it as the man with the clipboard left,' I say.

'Oh no!' she cries. 'You saw the loan-man?'

'Loan-man?'

'Please, please don't tell Harry. Please, he must not know that the loan-man calls. I'll do anything for you not to tell him.'

That was the wrong thing for a gorgeous young girl to say to an older girl who spent the late afternoon and the early evening amusing herself. 'Are you sure?' I ask. I put my finger on her chin, I can't believe that Rosa Saint John from last year would ever have dreamed of this or dared to attempt it, but ever so slowly I let my finger run down her neck, between her tits and right down to her navel. 'You'd do anything?'

'Yes,' she murmurs, 'Harry has a bad temper. He doesn't know about the loan-man.'

I flash my eyes. She's wonderfully submissive, means what she's said. I hook my finger at the top of her slacks to learn if she's going to cooperate. When I see Sally's hand reach for the door handle, I know I've got her. I walked backward, pulling her along with my finger tucked on her waistband. 'What are you going to do to me?' she asks pathetically.

'Make you realize that like most men, Harry is an asshole,' I say.

I lead her into the caravan, to the edge of the looping sofa, turn her to face me then ask her sweetly if she wants to remove my underwear. 'I'm nervous,' she whispers. 'I've never… You can take it off if you like.'

'This is a one-off,' I say gently, 'I'm not going to ask you to come in every time Harry goes out.'

'Thanks,' she says.

God, I'm so desperate for sex, so excited as I kick off my pants and undo my bra. Sally doesn't flinch. I think she can guess what I'm about to do.

As I gaze into her eyes, I take her pants off then ease her back onto the flat of the sofa. She's pale-skinned, hairless, I kneel between her legs and push her top and bra above her tits. 'You are beautiful,' I say as I begin to caress her body. She mutters a thank you completely unfazed by my wandering hands. And although I'm trembling with magnificent thrills Sally lays there motionless; she allows me total access to her flesh, gives me the freedom to seduce her with my fingers and tongue as not a single moan is released from her mouth. I fulfill myself, I bend her legs, raise them high, part them, do everything I dream of without her once giving a glimmer of resistance. There is a hint of a smile on her lips but no signs of extreme pleasure. Her scent is the sweetest of all. And when I've done, she merely says, 'Was that okay for you?' I lift her by the arms, kiss her with my stained lips and tell her that she's fabulous.

She gets dressed, reminds me that I've made a promise. 'If ever you're lonely,' I say as she exits the caravan. She leaves as if she's been to check on the water supply. For the first time in a long time, my body is somewhat satisfied, and my appetite for sex is gaining momentum.

**Let me down easy**

I was gazing in the mirror fixed to the tiny cupboard inside the caravan and wondering how a girl who formerly wouldn't instigate a handshake had transformed into one who'd take advantage of an innocent girl fearful of letting her man know that she borrows money.  Docile Rosa was now a vixen capable of preying on the vulnerable: duty and devotion mean shit – sex is my driving force and I intend to experience more.

Then I turned away, saw my phone on a window ledge.  It occurred to me that the short film of Brian is filed in the camera section.  Had Katy seen it when she checked my call register?  I wasn't sure; I needed to find out.

Katy appeared happy; she greeted me with a kiss close to the lips and bothered to show me an outfit she'd purchased from an internet store.  I told her about the brief visit to our parents and spent half an hour weighing up if I should make advances – I couldn't get sex out of my head but I didn't feel like it was going to happen here, at least, not today.

As I left, I cursed myself for telling Sally our sex had been a 'one-off'.  In retrospect, it should have been a down-payment on terms as lasting as her repayments to the loan-man.  There's not a doubt in my mind that the only person who can fulfill my needs is Tracey Cummings.  What's become of her?  What's become of the Queen of Whores who took me under her wing last summer?

**He was looking back to see if I was looking for a cup of tea**

As memories of our sexual exploits bubbled like volcanic lava in the mountainous regions I'd left in those heady few months of last year, I strode across the roads and pavements intent on catching at least a glimpse of Tracey Cummings' tiny figure on the dismal streets of the council estate.  She had to be somewhere…

I crossed over by the local shop that banned me, and almost got ran over by a car exceeding the speed limit of 20mph.  The car slowed.  A man's head stretches from the window.  'Rosa,' says a familiar voice.  I recognize the car.  Something swirls in my belly and I almost crease with the impact.  'Rosa!'

I reach the driver's door.  'Yes, Marty, I've returned.  Are you still breeding hedgehogs?'

He knows I'm referring to Caroline's pubic hair but fends off the remark with a grin.  'Can I make you a cup of tea?'

'Coffee, no sugar – have you forgotten?'

I get in the car and he drives me the short distance to the ex-matrimonial home.


**Partial Absolution**

I think of the return of the prodigal son.  I think of me sitting on all those South Coast beaches, licking ice-creams and truly believing I'd never see Marty or my family again.  He looks older than eight months older; there's stubble on his chin, he's staler than he used to be but he's acting like he's missed me and has hopes of some kind of reunion.

The first question I ask is about Caroline.  'Are you still subordinate to the office boss?' I say sarcastically.

He ignores me, goes straight to the kitchen to make the coffees, asks if I'd like a biscuit but so far, I'm not ready for intimacies.  He must be thinking too.  He stands waiting for the kettle to boil and it's probably three minutes before he comes back to the room and sits in his usual armchair.

'How are you?' he says. 'How long have you been back? Where have you been? Where are you living now?'

'I dossed around on the South Coast. You knew I couldn't stay in the house. How could I afford the bills? I had to go somewhere, didn't I?'

'Sorry,'' he says. Then he assembles his next statement carefully. 'I heard about your gang-bang at the Golf Club, it was gossip for ages, well, you and Tracey Cummings. I guess I drove you to it, my affair with Caroline, neglecting you, putting my requirements before yours. I've been a pig, Rosa. We had so much and I blew it.'

'You did,' I say reveling in his suffering. 'You couldn't accept that I didn't like Caroline one bit.'

'She's gone now. I learned that she went through the staff like a knife through butter. She's a user. I was one of her victims.'

'Poor you,' I say. 'You gave up all we had for a fucking fat slag with a bush at the top of her legs.'

'And you...' he says.

'Well, you know I slept around. I wanted to get back at you – wounded partner and all that – I'd have slept with the British Army if I thought you'd be hurt. You weren't even looking in my direction.'

'I went to the café to see if you were there,' he moans.

'The café closed.'

'I walked the streets trying to find you.'

'Good for you.'

'I've changed my job. I work for a computer firm.'

'I don't work at all.'

'Where are you living.'

'That would be telling.'

'Living alone?'

'Yes, me and my fingers.'

'So, you're not screwing around anymore.'

I fake a bout of laughter.  'What is sex?' I say.

'I ask the same question,' says Marty pathetically.

Then the conversation comes to an abrupt halt.  I look at the four walls and accept that once I was happy here; me the virgin who shacked up with an equally inexperienced guy whose only sin was to fall victim to a fat ugly creature with a hedgehog between her legs.  It all went wrong.  Sure, Marty learned a lesson but his lesson doesn't compare with what I've experienced.  He has no idea what heights I've climbed on Tracey Cummings' pink bedsheet or what other experiences have turned me on far more than he was ever able to accomplish.  He had his moments but feasting on Sally was more memorable than anything he ever did to me, apart from two things, two things that I did enjoy.

He coughs, then says meekly, 'You don't want to move in, do you?'

'You'd live with a whore,' I say.

'You're not a whore,' he says.

Out of meanness, I say, 'How would you like to screw my ass…?  After you've popped a couple of your little blue pills…  I take a lot of satisfying these days.'

He looks at me lovingly.  'I'd love to.'

I feel sorry for him; he's pitiful.  I think of our time together when I longed for him to grab my hair and drag me up the stairs, rip off my clothes and be as rough as possible.  He never did.  I don't wish to move in with him but I'm gagging to be screwed in ways that I choose.  Remember the cable ties on the landing,' I say.

'Sure,' he says.

'Remember the straps?'

'They're still in the bedroom drawer.'

I get to my feet.  'You need a shave.  I won't be moving in, but I'll call tonight around nine.  Maybe I'll let you loose on me.'

'Good of you, Rosa,' he says.  You'd think I'd offered to wash the dishes.


**I will get some satisfaction**

'If you don't treat me like a whore from the streets, I'm never coming back,' I tell Marty at one minute after nine.  'You heard about the gang-bang – that's what I want from you, mister.  I don't care in what state you leave me, but if you leave me with the strength to slap your face, I'll slap you violently, then walk out of here forever – got it?'

He looks shocked.  I go to our old drinks cabinet and find a half-full bottle of whiskey.  I plonk it on his lap and ask him how long the effects of his little blue pills will last.  He says they can keep him erect for two hours, sometimes.  I get out of a small bag I've brought with me a pair of leggings and a cotton top that's seen better days.  I tell him how it's got to be.  'I'll change into these.  I'll lay on the sofa and wait for you to drink the whiskey and take however many pills you like.  You're going to snatch a bunch of my hair and start to drag me around.  I'm going to fight you, kick you in the balls if you're not careful.  You're going to tear off my clothes, and I mean tear off my clothes.  And then you repeat what you did with the cable-ties and brutalize me on the landing, and if you're not rough enough, I'll bite off your dick, promise.  And then, if I'm not dead, you're cutting me free and taking me to our bed.  I want what you once did with the straps – remember?'

He remembers.

'And for the second hour, you're going to be worse than you were on the landing.  You're not to let up no matter what I say or how much I beg you to stop.  Is that clear, Marty?  Can you do it – if not, I'm going.  If not, you're no good for me.  Understand?'

I don't think he expected this.  He didn't anticipate how much I've changed since those days of domestic harmony.  I'm not sure if he's capable of doing what I've requested.  I tell him he's got a few minutes to think.  I go upstairs to change into my disposable clothing.  If I get half that I ask for it will be a better evening than laying on the sofa in the caravan.

When I return Marty is in the kitchen sipping whiskey from a small glass.  I relax on the sofa and slowly arrive at the conclusion he'll be a big disappointment.  What's new? – Marty is Marty and he lacks a sadistic streak.

He grunts and groans through the next ten minutes; I start thinking he's going to chicken out, apologize for his failings and ask if we can just be friends.  I call him, he doesn't answer then I lift my head and turn my shoulders.

He yells like a maniac, rags my hair and forces me onto the carpet.  As my face is pushed hard on the fibers he's already tearing at my top with his other hand.  I'm like a paper box, I didn't know he was so strong and my struggles are futile under the weight of his body.  He's taken off his clothes and swamping me with his flesh.  He rips off my top, hoists my bra over my head.  My head gets lifted and he slaps my face so hard that I want to scream.  I try to kick out; his knee presses down on my spine and my bottoms are torn to shreds.  We're seconds in and he's scaring me.  He twists me, pierces my tits with his fingernails before elevating me to my feet by the hair.  He doesn't allow me to stand upright but pushes my head to his crotch.  I'm being choked by his penis until seconds later I feel his fist land on the side of my head.  Oh God, this is brutal, I'm getting more than I asked for and his assault is cruel.  I shout, 'Marty' and receive a second blow to the head.

He doesn't even let me walk; he tosses my body from side to side until I lose balance, never letting go of my hair and inflicting heavy slaps on my back and ass.  I'm pulled up the stairs like a sack of potatoes at the end of a short leash.  My flesh rubs on the stair carpet and I feel burn marks.  I'm hurting, feeling so much pain that I no longer struggle.  I gasp for air and see my arms flop below my head as he slings me over the landing railing.  I manage to say 'please' but the slaps rain on me like I'm not supposed to speak.  He calls me a whore and I get a half-powered punch in the ribs.  Then he cable-ties me to the railing just like once before, but then he respected me, then I was still his partner and the docile girl he set up home with.  He heaves on my limbs, stretches me while I scream and I vainly use my feeble energy in attempts to repel him.  It is useless.  I'm separated as easily as twigs, bound by my ankles and wrists to places on the railing I thought were impossible to reach.  He jerks on my hair as if he's trying to break my neck and enters me from behind as viciously as he is able.  With that initial thrust comes my first erotic sensation; I think back to the Golf Club and recall what I did to survive.  Let it happen, soak up the pain, accept gratefully whatever I receive, know this is sex most vile and most rewarding.  He pumps into me like an out of control piston.  I start to moan, start to sense that my body is capable of anything.  And as he did before he comes to the tops step and screws my mouth but now, he doesn't seem to care if I live or die.  I can't breathe, I can't cry for him to stop.

Again, and again, from behind and into my mouth; my scalp yields to soreness, my body stings as slaps are ceaseless; I know I have an orgasm but it passes so quickly that I scarcely appreciate its luxury.  Marty is possessed by the devil.  He's challenging for the top spot in my memory.  He's driving so far inside me I think he'll rupture me.  On and on for what seems like an eternity until he uses his fist between my legs.  And when he cuts me free, he catches me as I collapse then once more drags me by the hair and heaves my scarred body onto the bed.  Did I tell him to be so violent?  Is this what I asked for believing it would happen?

He straps my wrists to my ankles then just as I ordered lays me on my back.  He crushes my thighs in his grip; he pounds his open hand rapidly on my pussy and orders me to cum and he won't proceed until I have done.  Help me.  Help me.  Then he blindfolds me and his request is fulfilled.  He attacks again, pressing on my knees and distressing my hips.  I begin to feel a continuous spasm of ecstasy; my body is frying and juices are flowing but they don't extinguish the fire.  'Marty, you bastard!' 'Screw me harder!'  'Is that all you've got?'

He slaps me, scratches me, digs into my flesh with his fingertips and keeps on tearing at my wettened hair.  But I sense that he can't go on.  I sense that his will to defeat me is waning.  I sense that I've taken all that he can give and he's little left in reserve.  I goad him, 'I thought you were screwing me.  I'm just getting going.'

I force him to prolong his efforts.  He slaps my face harder than before, drives into me as if he's trying to show he's not done, but he is done, he is weakening, he is shuddering to a stop and just as when the gang-bang finished I feel elated. I have survived, and Marty rolls to my side in exhaustion.

I ask him to undo the straps. He barely has strength but manages to free me. I take off the blindfold and see the wretched state of my body then feel my swollen face and the forming bruises on my limbs. Oh yes, I'm weak, still pouring, still tingling and more satisfied than I ever imagined I could be. 'See what you can do when you try,' I say.

Marty snuggles his face against my breasts. 'Did I pass the test?'

'Borderline,' I say, 'maybe you'll get a re-run.


## A long recovery

Maybe I gave the impression that the sex with Marty was normal. I goaded Marty; this wasn't the type of sex I'd advocate, not for ordinary folk, not for those with a healthy disposition. It was sex that I'd fantasized about since Tracey first bound me to metal rods; the violence, those heavy slaps and punches were extras, born from Marty's interpretation of my description. I've never been hurt like that, never needed time to recover or time to let my scars heal. I was taken through two hours of hell at my request. That's who I've become, the ultimate victim of brutality and the complete antithesis of the girl who licked her way into Sally's memory.

At two in the morning, I got a cab to the top of Katy's street and hobbled to the caravan, carrying my pains and fading pleasures on legs made of jelly and with my insides throbbing like a bass drum. Of course, I stripped naked and lay on my narrow bed with the light dimmed.  I couldn't move for hours, I felt like I'd been in a boxing ring with a heavyweight.  The aftereffects were ten times worse than the gang-bang but I didn't regret being dominated so decisively.  Pain and pleasure are twins and I love them both.

When I failed to call at Katy's during the day, she found an excuse to give Brian to sneak out in the evening and come to the caravan.  I'd not moved, well, only once or twice.  Katy found me sprawled open-legged on the bed.  She was horrified seeing the state of me.  I told her I'd had rough sex with a stranger, something I needed to do because I felt unloved, rejected, kind of alone in the world and I desired physical action.  I thought she'd go berserk, but she didn't; a mild chastisement came with a whole lot of tenderness.

She asked if there was anything she could do to help.  I begged her to soothe me, soothe me how all women soothe themselves when nights are cold and lonely.  Yes, I repeated myself many times, pleading with her to understand that a gentle sin is a gift to heal those suffering.  She was reluctant, at first patted my skin until I took her hand and directed its fingers to where they should go.  And when she overcame her reticence her movements were easier and she began to smile knowing she comforted me.

The next morning, she returned to comfort me again, and then again in the afternoon.  And by the next day, I'd convinced her that we'd come a long way with our expressions of love.  Perhaps there is more to life than housekeeping for Brian and being the mother of two school-age children.  I promised her adventures and she said she'd consider my offer.

Very late on that final evening, Katy phoned me.  She whispered.  I could barely hear her.  She wanted to know the secret.  She wanted to know what I'd been keeping from her that related to Brian.


## Considering my options

The final few hours I spent walking on Brighton beach were filled with conjecture over a return to Leeds.  Where I would head to when my feet landed on the platform of the railway station, who I'd first see, first talk with, where I'd rest my head, and who'd be the first to give intimacy?  In fractions of thought, my guesses changed.  Hope lay with Tracey Cummings.  Practicality lay with Marty.  Likelihood may be with Katy.  If all else failed, perhaps then my parents.

But now, one week after my return, I am no clearer with my thoughts; sexual longing steers me to where sex is available, my heart craves for Tracey, and to some extent Katy, yet it would be so uncomplicated and easy to renew my relationship with Marty.  Not that I'd goad him to beat me again and leave me wounded; as with the Golf Club, that evening was a one-off, a kind of trophy to carry to old age.  Marty is a wimp of a guy; he'd never have done that to me before Caroline, not even with encouragement.

Realistically, at this moment only two options are available – I stay here in the caravan or go back to Marty.  When I add Katy to a second possible encounter with Sally, to the freedom to pursue Tracey Cummings, the caravan wins.  I'm sorry, Marty, but my love for you is not what it used to be.

**A new agreement**

Most of the scars have vanished; there's a little swelling on my jaw and one or two bruises in sensitive areas, but I'm back to normal and ready for some kind of action. I've got to say, the more days that I go without sex, the less it preoccupies my thinking. If I pass another day on my back in the caravan I'll be sending for magazines or becoming a fan of soap operas on the television. I've no wish to go back to my exile habit of mostly being celibate.

Katy texts to tell me to drop in; she says a surprise is waiting. Hell, I hope she's wearing sexy lingerie holding a pair of handcuffs and a vibrator the length of a telegraph pole. I'm coming, Katy. I see Harry as I shut the caravan door; he gives me a look that says he wishes he dared to speak. I say, 'Hi', he blushes and nods, then hurries over to his motorbike.

I go to Katy's, go straight to the kitchen where she's standing close to the kettle ready to make a coffee. She looks fabulous in a tight-fitting dress with matching shoes with moderately high heels. As she's been kind to me these past days, I reward her with a kiss that leaves nothing to the imagination. We hug each other's ass and I tell her I love her.

She loves me too; she's loved me all my life. She makes the coffee and we sit facing each other on tall stools with nice padded tops. 'Was that my surprise?' I say.

'Partly,' she says. Then she acquires a serious expression and asks what I think of Brian, her husband.

She knows I despise him, always have, always will. I can't be as blunt as I want to be so I use a euphemism. 'He's not my type. I don't like over-confident guys.'

'That day,' begins Katy, 'when we watched the film of you being gang-banged at the Golf Club, the film from Brian's phone, you threatened me with your phone, then you stopped threatening me and left.  You have something on Brian and I want to know what it is.'

'I'd never hurt you, Katy,' I say.

'Didn't your sex escapade begin after Marty screwed his boss?  Isn't all that you've done since, a kind of revenge?  If Brian has done to me what Marty did to you, I swear I'll go along the same path even though it's not in my nature to be disloyal.'

This is so difficult.  I'm torn – I think I have a chance of getting Katy in bed but I'd hate to hurt her.  'He told you he left the Golf Club immediately.  He didn't.  The film is from the beginning to the end.  And he got close to the action, didn't he?'

'Are you saying he was one of those who screwed you, Rosa?'

'No, I don't believe he did.  I think he got very close, but not that close.'

'Tell me... tell me what you've got on him.'

'I can't.'

'If you do, I promise you I'll have sex with another man.'

'What about me?' I say.

'It's wrong,' she says.

'It's only a little further to go than we've already been.'

'You're my sister.  I want to know about Brian – what's he done?  I won't tell him I know.  I'll do what you did.  You can take me out and get some guy to...'

I rise from the stool and attempt to kiss Katy and fondle her body.  'I want you,' I say a dozen times.  She won't let me take her to her bedroom, instead just keeps on promising that she'll let me take her somewhere to be fucked.  This is a terrible decision.

She sees my phone on the work surface, pleads again to view the evidence.

I show her the short film of Brian outside my house, below my bedroom window. It's a day or two after the gang-bang. He's called to have sex with me. He thinks I'm an easy target but I don't let him in. I'm hanging out of the window and he's feeling his balls. When I reject him, he leaves and the footage ends with the lens sweeping over my naked tits.

'I'm not shocked,' says Katy.

'If only it had been you,' I say. Now she allows me to kiss her as I wanted to before. She allows me to let my hands wander over her body. I bite her neck, use all the tricks I know to seduce her, but she only allows me to go so far.

'We've agreed. Find me a man. I want revenge. I'll do what you did but maybe not go beyond one act of betrayal.

'Can't it be with me?' I begged.

'No, Rosa, at least not yet.'


**A fortuitous encounter**

Katy leaves me hanging. I walk from the private estate through the small wood to come out at the top boundary of the field. I see old friends Miranda and Genni but they quicken their pace so as not to talk to me – I'm an outcast, one of those girls even semi-decent girls don't wish to be associated with. Tracey Cummings and Rosa Saint John have a lot in common.

Another visit to Tracey's door has me thinking she could have moved on, maybe she's become a star in porn movies, maybe that rich American, Herman, who she services once in a while, has taken her to California to be his plaything. Through her window, nothing inside looks different, but Tracy is capable of upping sticks and leaving empty-handed.

I get the bright idea to call at Geoff's house. When I first decided to get some sex lessons away from Marty, it was Tracey who arranged my meeting with his sons. Geoff may know of Tracey's whereabouts and when my body's pining for her attention I don't mind if Geoff demands that I sit on his lap.

He answers the door looking as frail as ever, as miserable as ever, and he has to stare for a minute before he recognizes me. I ask him if he's seen Tracey. 'She'll be laid on her back somewhere,' he says. I don't get invited inside but suddenly Kev leaps down the stairs and claims that he heard my voice.

'Where's your girlfriend?' I say.

'The girlfriends only turn up in the afternoon,' says Kev. 'Timmy's and mine are sisters.'

I think on my feet; I'm trying to assess if Katy would be brave enough to partake of the same double-up as mine last year. Cheekily I say, 'Do you still have the black cloth bag that you place on a girl's head?'

'Sure,' says Kev.

'Are you up for doing my sister a favor,' I say. 'You and Timmy.'

He laughs. 'Your sister's a tart too?'

'Training,' I say.

'Bring her here in the morning,' says Kev, 'but don't bother if she's ugly or unfit.'

I smile to myself, walk back to the field thinking I've had a small achievement. I cut through the small wood and head back to my caravan wondering what I can do for the next couple of hours. It's a warm day and the sun is shining. At this time of year, birds are breeding, and I'm jealous because today the only body I can breed with belongs to me.

I tidy the interior, let the warmth flood in through the open door, and spend a few minutes cursing myself for not pressing the issue about sleeping with Katy.  She'd have submitted to my demands if I'd withheld the film for another hour.  She can't know that revenge tastes sweeter with a man when she hasn't tasted a member of the same sex.  Her ideas are old-fashioned and it's time she got modern ideas.

I start sulking, walk up and down the narrow central space and notice that I've not yet emptied the bin.  I pull out the lining and stumble as I'm heading out to the dustbin; the rubbish spills and I bend down to pick it up.

Then who appears... sweet little Sally comes from her door in a colorful kimono carrying a similar-size bag of rubbish. She puts her bag in the main bin then comes over to help me.  'I'm always dropping mine,' she says.  I think she can drop them for me any day.  I smile before plonking my bag on top of her bag in the main bin.  I see her bare feet and think how pretty they'd look trapped in the straps of the arced sofa (there's a looped strap on each cushion probably to allow for cleaning beneath the individual seats).

'Hey, that suits you,' I say.

As ever, she's as timid as a mouse.  'Oh, thank you.'

Today's Rosa Saint John isn't shy in coming forward. 'What are you wearing under it?'

'Nothing,' murmurs Sally.

We gaze open-eyed.  I time my next question perfectly. 'Did you enjoy the other day?'

She blushes faintly, lowers her eyes, 'It was nice.'

'And if the opportunity came along... is Harry at work?'

'He is,' she says.  I detect one of her legs twitch.  I'm screaming at myself to go for it.  I focus on the kimono belt, take a step closer and hook my finger just below her navel on the knot.

'Are you leaving your door open?' I say and she knows what I mean.  I give her a moment to think before releasing her.

She closes her door then precedes me into the caravan.  I tell her how I've dreamed of being with her again.  I offload compliments with ridiculous frequency.  She just lurks in front of the sofa expecting me to do what I did to her last time.  God, I'm horny.  Unforeseen sex gets the juices flowing instantly.

I wrap my hands around her waist, press against her tiny ass and whisper in her ear.  'I love your body.  Do you love mine?'

She stammers as she says 'Yes'.  I undo her belt, then pull the collar from her shoulders and let the kimono fall to the floor.  I'm behind her.  I'm enormously aroused and seeing her naked sends shivers down my spine.  She's expecting me to turn her, let her fall on the seat, then I'll go down on her.  She's about to discover that sex with a girl like me is a two-way partnership.  I take off my clothes, rub my tits on her back and run my tongue across her shoulders.  The second her arms stray from her body I lift her bottom onto the sofa and carefully place one foot through a loop attached to a cushion.  She is silent, lets me do as I wish.  I miss out on one loop and stretch her, just managing to secure her ankle in the next loop for easier access.  I lay her back with the top third of her body dangling from the rim of the sofa.  It's the most stunning sight I've seen since putting Tracey Cummings in Marty's straps before devouring her.

I stand over her head and am unable to resist speaking dirty to her;  I tell her I'm going to poke her until she begs for more, and then I'll lower my face where it's requested and I'll lower myself onto her face and she must copy what I do.  Sally's expression speaks of innocence.  Her body is young, fresh, palely pink and white.  Her vibrating thighs are glorious and patience dies within me.  I sink on her, please her using all the skills I've learned from Tracey and quench my lust in the tight pure folds of her youthfulness.  Oh, this sex is a universe apart from that I shared with Marty.  I feel so alive, so perfectly attracted to a girl's flesh that there isn't a fiber of me that goes without bliss;  I drown in her luscious release, I wait for her call to comfort me, and when she cries I am ready to accept her virgin licks and the soft embraces of her face.  This is sex untainted. sex that allows the soul to glow in happy satisfaction, sex that produces an endless beautiful orgasm that runs through the veins like an angel's breath.  The sensations are indescribable, they occur effortlessly, naturally, and the mind glides on an ocean of thrills seamlessly to utter ecstasy.


**Marty calls me**

'It's been a few days,' he says.
        'I've been busy,' I say.
        'Have you recovered?'
        'From what?'
        'The sex.'
        I pause before answering as if the sex with him was forgettable.  'Oh, that sex.  Yes, I'm fine.'
        'Are you busy now?' he says.
        'I'm taking a shower then going to bed.'
        'Call any time,' says Marty.
        'Sure, good to hear from you.'

**I call…**

I sit thinking about Sally and Harry; they remind me of Marty and me from two years ago.  So little sexual experience is not always a recipe for success.  If I'd known the pleasures of an older woman or even a well-traveled man, I'd have been aware of what I was taking on when I told Marty our relationship was for life.  A part of me knows that I'm interfering by doing what I do with Sally, but another part of me believes I'm educating her, broadening her outlook on life before her beauty begins to fade and she becomes cynical as life's pressures mount.  I could never love a girl like Sally; she's porcelain, too fragile to be more than exquisite.  She wouldn't respond to roughness and after a dozen sessions with her, I'd be bored.

It could be that Katy is similar.  I'll put her to the test.  She seems to accept that Brian is no longer that husband to adore.  I hope she's true to her word.

And then there is Tracey Cummings… voices in my head keep scolding me for not calling her.  But the voices don't realize that if I call Tracey and she answers, and I ask to meet her, and she tells me she's not interested… what then?

She ended our relationship because she couldn't bear the pain of love.  Over a telephone you don't see pain in the caller's eyes, nor do you see truth.  And that's why I haven't called her.

I smash into a moment of weakness and call her.  The phone rings.  She does not answer.

I feel relieved.  I'm determined to hunt her down.  I want to see her in the flesh and ask her if she loves me.

**Up yours, Brian!**

Katy drops in at the caravan; she appears determined to distance herself from Brian.  Once more I go over the events at the Golf Club and his subsequent visit to my former home.  She confesses to old suspicions about his behavior; there was no-one to tell, we weren't close then, maybe we should have been.

When she's on the sofa I deliver another of my kisses, and although she responds she shakes her head immediately afterward and makes it clear that's as far as we go.  'You don't know what you're missing out on,' I say jokingly.  But Katy's adamant that lesbian sex isn't for her.

I tell her we'll go visit our parents; they'll be shocked to see us together.  We can call at a shop for provisions and I need to pop in on a friend at the council estate.  Katy is casually dressed, and her mood brightens once we start walking and the threat of me pouncing on her as gone.  I pinch her bottom a few times and tease her.  'I'm going there one of these days,' I say, and slowly a 'no' changes to a 'maybe' which encourages me to be even cheekier.

I pretend not to care where we go first and she thinks we should get the visit to our parents out of the way.  I keep her chatting and we inadvertently take the wrong path through the small wood and come out at the very top corner of the field.  'It's easier to go to my friend's house first,' I say.  'I'll only be five minutes.'

Katy smiles, she's in no hurry, but she does ask me my friend's name.  I'm tongue-tied as I search for a name, spit out Georgia but it doesn't sound correct, and Katy notices.

'You're not up to mischief, Rosa.'

'Cross my heart and hope to die,' I say. 'It's still morning – who gets up to mischief this early?'

'You get up to mischief any time of day.'

I lead her to the cul-de-sac and tell her that we've arrived. Katy follows me up the short path to Geoff's front door. I tap lightly. Geoff opens the door and says softly, 'Come in, girls.'

I proceed along the hallway and signal to Katy to wait for me when she gets half-way. She stops. I follow Geoff into the end room. I glance back at Katy and she is smiling sweetly. I count in my head 'I... 2... 3... 4... 5...'

Kev and Timmy leap on her from behind and place the cloth bag over her head; they pull the string that secures it, and just as they did with me all those months ago, they lift her horizontally before tilting her to a 45-degree angle at the bottom of the stairs, then she is gone, struggling, and I hear her muffled screams fading as they take her up to a bedroom.

I know what they'll do to her; my lovely sister is unprepared, unwarned and likely trembling with fear. Those first minutes are the worst when you're not sure if it's sudden death or slow death. You see life flashing by, you dread your throat being slashed or something equally barbaric. You squeal inside as they rip off your clothes and expose your body to their omnipotence. Geoff sits in his chair and minds his own business. I lean against a sideboard and pray that Katy will understand.

Understand! Now that's a ridiculous word for such a situation. My God, what have I done to her?

It's like I can hear screams and cries and gasps for breath. I'm wanting to race upstairs and be her substitute. Did she mean it when she said she'd cheat on Brian? Some folks say things without real intention. 'She's gone quiet,' mumbles Geoff as if telling me she's died.

Then there is clattering, bangs on the upstairs floorboards and I know that Katy's ordeal is ending.  I watch the hallway and see her head appear inside the black cloth bag.  Kev and Timmy are carrying her naked body, and crudely I enjoy the moment because this is the first occasion that I've seen her body since we went through puberty.  They take her to the rear door, toss her into the garden as if she's an old carpet.  I yell, 'Where are her clothes?'  Timmy runs back upstairs, comes down with torn garments and throws them at Katy; she's distressed, I scramble toward her and cuddle her in my arms.

The rear door slams.  She's crying, covered in the brother's squirts of pleasure.  Her arms are flailing and making it hard for me to dress her and the rips in her clothes don't make covering her easy.

I pull her to her feet and we scramble past the high gate.  I force her to run because her body is on show – no knickers, as they left me, no bra and a top ripped to shreds.  Her pants cover most of her legs but not her private area.  As we run, she rubs her ass as though it is hurting.  'Keep going,' I say, 'let's make it to the wood.'

As we reach the edge of the wood I glance over my shoulder and on the opposite side of the field close to the shelter I notice a bus slowing.  I see Tracey Cummings running for the bus. Oh god, my lover, my sister in chaos – where do I turn?  What do I do?

Katy dives into the trees and I follow her.  She squats in a clump of tall grass.  I embrace her, apologize to her.  She tells me it was the most horrific experience of her life – I can't imagine what they did to her.  'Both of them?' I say.

'Everywhere, and I mean everywhere.  I'm wet, in pain, and my insides are battered.'

I kiss her head, say, 'Sorry, sorry, sorry.'

'I can't walk the streets like this,' she moans.

I offer to run to the caravan, bring her clothes to protect her modesty.  She instantly agrees and off I go.

When I return ten minutes later Katy is calmer.  She puts on my jeans and a top over the torn items.  We hurry to her house, flop against the work surface in the kitchen supported by our outstretched arms.  We pant, kind of shiver with relief.  'I'm so sorry,' I say again.

'You're not going to believe it,' says Katy, 'that was sensational – I loved it.  What they did to me was unreal.  I orgasmed, properly orgasmed for the first time in my life.'

We fall into each other's arms and she allows me to fondle her without a hint of complaint.  Once more I'm optimistic; I don't care if she's just been through a mind-blowing experience, I want to put her through another.  And when Katy mentions a shower, I smother her in kisses and offer to run the water.  She agrees.  Minutes later and I'm watching her coat her body in soap; her body is much like mine but elongated, tinier tits but lovely shaped hips that dazzle the eye.

Can I join her?  Let's have sex in the shower,' I suggest.

She offers me her hand, pulls me toward her and kisses my lips.  'Maybe some other time, sis.  Right now, I'm lapping up my act of revenge.'


**What's going on?**

Some evenings, I can lay on my bed or the sofa for a couple of hours and not feel horny.  Other times I do naughty things.  Right now, I wonder if I'm becoming a sex maniac – worse than Tracey –

because names of potential victims are streaming through my mind.  I want sex with someone and I'm not particularly bothered who comes along.

Why doesn't Katy kick Brian into touch?  Why doesn't Sally get Harry to work 24 hours a day to pay off the loan she hasn't told him about?  Why doesn't Marty call and say he's thought of a method of sexual intercourse that no-one in the history of evolution has tried?  More desperately, I think Kev and Timmy should ditch their girlfriends and practice their black hood routine three times an hour on my body.  I'm so lonesome that if I had any of Marty's little blue pills then I may go stuff a handful down old Geoff's throat – that would get him going, and me going too.

And of course, the best prize of all would be a three-hour session with Tracey.  All those times we screwed for the sake of screwing; all those tricks she knew and her two drawers filled with toys, all the pleasure she gave me outweighs the total pleasure of my life.  And yes, I haven't forgotten that she got on a bus; she's alive and kicking – that's a start.

One thing that didn't strike me when I saw her but strikes me now is that she wasn't dressed like a whore, well, not as outlandish as she used to dress; perhaps she's become a one-at-a-time girl.  I'd hate to think that she's got a boyfriend.

I'm thinking of going on the prowl.  Rosa Saint John – yes, I'll hold my hands up – is a slag.


**Late night, deserted streets, couples in bed, a walk in the park**

I stop thinking about going out on the prowl, I go out on the prowl with the belief that if I wander long enough in my local area then

I'll find some guy or some lonely girl in need of a bit of comfort. Look how successful Tracey used to be, or still is; there have been so many notches carved on her gun that the barrel has dropped off.

Selfishly, I blame Katy for this flood of frustration. If she'd have shared the shower water, I may now be looking forward to Brian going to work and the kids going to school. I'd show her some tricks of my own in her double bed, I'd make the memory of Kev and Timmy look like a crisp at the side of a feast. I'd be stuffing Brian's socks inside her mouth to prevent her from screaming. When am I going to get lucky? Oh, shut up, I know I got lucky with Sally - so what!

I amaze myself. I go to the lane behind the church and wander like a lost pigeon, in circles, to and fro, with my hands clasped on my ass as though I'm an old librarian. Doesn't the priest walk his dog if he has a dog? Don't randy drunks pass this way going home from the pub? I'm only 300 yards from Marty but the problem is with Marty is that I know what I'll get. Presently, I'm not keen on knowing what I'm going to get – some kind of ghastly surprise would be a treat: six teenage girls going to an orgy or a lads' night out in need of entertainment. This lane seems to be closed to pedestrians.

Then the council estate looks like a graveyard. Tracey Cummings' house is in darkness. The only lights are in couples' bedrooms where they're trying shagging to be seen for the first time. If I had a fist on a long pole I may knock on some upstairs windows and ask if anyone is open to a threesome. Shit! Why don't I just go home?

Marty or me and my fingers?

I leave the estate via a road that goes in a very long curve and passes the park a short distance from the top of Katy's street.

There are two pubs on the way that are usually busy; at this time of night the punters are wandering home to their wives, but not all of them have wives and a pretty young girl is a night-time attraction.  And what do I see? – three ancient men and an old girl on a mobility scooter.

If I goad Marty enough, can I again turn him into a monster?

The park gates are open which comes as a mild surprise.  I fantasize about laying naked on one of the benches, fantasize about skinny-dipping in the small lake but the water will be freezing and it takes the heater in the caravan a while to warm.  I cut through a path between neatly pruned trees; it's pitch-black, I suddenly stop because I think I hear feet shuffling close by.

The next thing I know is that I'm face-down on the ground and the blade of a knife is pressing on my cheek.  A man's voice is issuing instructions, 'Don't move, don't make a sound, fucking do as I say and you won't get hurt.'

He starts writhing at my knickers, forcing my body to bend.  Am I frightened – not as frightened as I thought I'd be being raped?  He keeps on swearing, pulling my hair, heaving up my skirt and growling like an angry bear.  Madly, I want to tell him he can have sex for free but there's something in his voice that appalls me.  I don't struggle.  I let him get on with it and I sense that he's shocked by my lack of fear.  He thinks I'm a stranger.  He can't keep going for much more than a minute and when he delivers his final threat, I know he's going to run off.  As he runs off, I lift my head and see a shadow disappearing behind the trees.  I add the shape of the shadow to the voice and nod with certainty.  I always knew he was a slimy bastard.  That's not the first rape in this park in recent times.  And now I know the rapist's identity – my sister is married to a rapist, and his name is Brian.

**Quick question...**

The next morning after she'd completed the school-run, I pop into Katy's and ask her if she had a row with Brian last night.

'How did you know?'

'I saw him stomp up the street.  I wondered if you'd told him you'd had a big one up each hole.'

Katy laughed.  'Not at all, but I did tell him that I'm thinking of divorcing him.'

'Good for you, Katy,' I said.  'I'll catch you later.'

I have a civic duty to report Brian to the police, but who would the police believe if his fellow upstanding members of the Golf Club spoke up for him.  'Hey, that's the girl we gang-banged last year; she loves sex, we were all in the park showering her with affection.'


**Marty wants me home**

I'm not shaken by the event in the park but I feel like a normal conversation wouldn't go amiss.  My parents are no use, and the only person I can think of who'll listen to me is Marty. Fortunately, his car is on the drive.  And when he sees me, he's welcoming, offers a coffee and a sandwich if I'm hungry.  Sure, he asks again where I am living but I refuse to tell him – it's not my house and the owners don't like people they don't know calling. What do I do all day?  I tell him I'm idle, read magazines, clean up for the couple who rent me a room, and spend half my time wishing I still worked in the café with Josivini.  The impression of a lonely inactive girl goes down well.  Marty does a lot of smiling

and he tells me about his new job, it's interesting and keeps his
thoughts focused on what's important.

He says he didn't mean to hurt me when we had sex but
he believed that's the kind of sex I wanted.  I tell him he rose to
new heights.  If he can come up with any suggestions that may
tingle my taste-buds, then text me.  I'm not averse to having sex
with him, I just like being free; for the time being, I like being free
– who knows what will change.

Marty asks me to come home.  He doesn't plead because
he knows that would antagonize me.  I promise I may stay for a
night, especially if his sex suggestions are noteworthy.  Then we
chat about the weather and lots of other meaningless crap which
does something to heal the rift of the past.  Hey. I'm still quite
fond of him but he's some distance behind Tracey Cummings and
Katy, and sex-wise, give me a double portion of Sally any day of
the week.


**Minor/Major progress – who knows?**

Two days go by; more reconnaissance trips to Tracey Cummings'
house, more erotic fantasies about both Katy and Sally, and at
least a dozen descriptive talks with Katy about how I can make her
feel like a complete woman.  Marty has come up with nothing
alluring and I'm beginning to think of running into the center
circle of an active football match and blowing a whistle.  'Get
stuck in lads – a different kind of practice is open!'

However, I've been scheming... I've done nothing about it,
apart from not washing the knickers I wore on the night in the
park – but scheming is the correct word.  I've dreamed up a plan
to put more than the shits up Brian's windpipe and thus get Katy

all to myself.  Yes, this is bitchy, callous, but didn't I say that I have a civic duty?  Brian deserves his comeuppance and with good fortune, that's exactly what he's going to get.

This is the plan: Brian comes home from work in his car via the main road at the very top of Katy's street.  5.30, regular as clockwork.  He always drives slowly towards the houses because sometimes kids are playing on the footpaths.  So… I offer Kev and Timmy twenty quid apiece to wait with me at the roadside so when Brian's car chugs towards us they can block its path and halt it.  Now it's my turn.  I knock on the driver's window.  Brian wonders what's going on.  I grin, tell him he's the biggest bastard in Northern England and I'm going to bring him to his knees.  He'll fucking laugh at me, I'm sure of that.  Then I take from a brown paper bag my semen-stained knickers and say, 'Hey, buster, your DNA is on these pants from that night you raped me in the park. If you haven't disappeared from this city in 24 hours, me, Kev and Timmy are going to the police station.'

Foolishly he asks if Kev and Timmy were in the park.

'24 hours, or you're locked up for fifteen years.'

We clear the road and allow him to drive on.  Fantastic, eh?  Who's going to be snuggling up to Katy in a day or two?


**Plan aborted due to decisive action**

This is exactly what happened, not a morsel of exaggeration nor any bending of the truth – withholding of a truth or two, maybe, but everyone is allowed secrets.

My nose was going blue between the blinds of the rear caravan window.  I'd been willing Harry to go out on his motorbike.  I'd made up my mind, if he did so, I vowed to hammer on Sally's door and tell her if she didn't get her ass exposed on my sofa inside two minutes then I'd pick up her ass, bare it on her doorstep and have her stripped naked before she could blink a single eyelid. I wanted her body. I'd been imagining it aching for the best part of two hours and I was in no mood to not make it ache. 'Sally, I'm going to have sex with your pale pink flesh whether you want sex or not.'

Please, Harry, go for a five hundred mile ride while I ride your young wife.

The handle turns on my door. Katy walks in with her girls. My eyes fall from their sockets and roll across the carpets (sorry, that's an exaggeration, isn't it?). She's brought her girls – call an ambulance!

Katy is happy, she renewed their lost memories and introduced me as Aunty Rosa. The girls confess to remembering me; I once bought them computer games and worked in a café. Katy invites me to her house. Do I wish to go when Brian is there? – like hell, I don't.

'Come,' Katy insists, 'there's only me and the girls.' We can indulge in a snack and several hours of chat. I'm disappointed, I'm seldom chatty in bed. However, I go to spend my curiosity over a coffee and a ginger biscuit.

Katy chats happily, about the girls' schoolwork, the clothes she buys them, flowers in her garden, the price of cooked ham, and a million other essential topics. I'm bemused and wonder if I'll be here when her kids go to bed. There is no rush to dispose of me and still no sign of Brian.

At 9, the kids go to bed. At 10, she lets her mask fall from her face. 'He's gone... gone for good... I've told him that I don't love him anymore and that our relationship is dead.'

'Dead!' I say.

'Dead, never to be resurrected,' she says.

There follows a period of comforting; holding hands, listening to the reasons why her love died. She's reviewed the film of my gang-bang and had convinced herself that Brian came too close for him not to resist. And coming to my house when my breasts were exposed. 'I believe he'd have burst in if your door had been unlocked,' she said. 'He often asked me to do things that I wouldn't. Quite honestly, I hate him. I never want to see him again.'

Katy asked me to stay the night. 'What, in your bed?'

'In my bed,' she said then made it clear there wouldn't be what I hoped there'd be. 'You can love me, oh, I don't mind you loving me.'

A crumb is better than starving – one raindrop brings a little wetness.

Almost midnight we go to bed. Almost midnight when ghosts come out to play and most eyes are sleeping. Katy tells me about the final straw that broke the back of her marriage. I'm filled with inquisitiveness. 'Final straw?' I say.

'He went for a walk to the park after we'd had a blazing row,' she begins. 'Nothing special about that, he's done it before.'

'There have been rapes in that park,' I say. She ignored me.

'The morning after, I found his underwear in the laundry basket. His boxer shorts were stained. I think he'd had sex and it wasn't with me.'

Oh God, please tell me what to say next. Katy sees me shuddering. I can't help myself but tears start flooding from my eyes. 'Rosa, Rosa,' she says holding me to her breast.

'I was raped in the park. I was jumped from behind. I never saw his face but I heard him threaten me.'

'It was Brian?' murmurs Katy.  'I just know it was Brian.
Did he recognize you?'

'I don't think so.  I was just a girl walking alone.  He took
his chance.  That's it.'

I feel more loved than at any time in my life because Katy
doesn't doubt my story.  She loves me like the big sister I've
always desired.  More than that, she leads me to her bedroom
and pulls back the duvet.  She tells me to undress.  I must lay with
my arms still.  I must not think this is sex but merely a reward she
gifts to me.

When I lay there, I taste happiness.  When I lay there, I
float through the most serene moments of existence.  I shall keep
my secret.  I shall conceal the truth in my heart for the remainder
of my life.


**And then...**


When Katy returned from her school trip X XXX XXX XXXX.  X
XXXXXXXXXXX XXX XXX XXXXXXXX XXX XXXXXXXX XXX XXXXX.  X
XXXXX XXXX XXX, XXXXXXX XXXXXXXXXX X XXXX, XXXX XXXXXX XX
XXX XXXX, XXXXXX XXX, XXXXX XXX, XXXXXXXX XXX, XXX XXXXXX
XXX XXXXXX XXXXXXX XXXX XXXXXX XXXXXX XXXXX XXXX XX'X
XXXX.  X XXXXXXXX XXX XXX, XXXXXXXX XXX XXXX XXXXXXXX
XXXXXXX XXX XXXX XXX XXX XXXX XX XXXX.

XX XXX, X XXXXXX XXX XXXX X'X XXXXXX XXXXXX.  X XXXXX
XXX XXX XXXX XXX XXXX XXX XXXXXXXXX XXX XXXXX XXXX
XXXXXXXX.  X XXXX XXX XXX XX XX XXXX, XXXX XXX XXXX XXX XXXX
XX XXX XXXXXX XX XXXX XXXX XXXXXXXXXX.  X XXXXXXXXX XX XXX.
X XXXXXXXX XXX XXX XX XXXXXXX XX XXX.  XX XXXXXX XXXX XXXXX

XXXXXX, XXXXXXXXXX, XXX XXXXXXX XXXX XXXXX'X XXXXX XXXXX XXXX XXXX XXX XXXXX XXX XXXX.


## Accepting the changes

When Marty left for Caroline's before my exile to the South Coast, I wasn't broken or distraught, nevertheless, a change had come; I lived in the house alone and the silence took some getting used to.  There were other marked differences – one meal to make, one seat occupied, a half-empty bed, no voice answering my questions, and even though we weren't touchers the mere thought of not being touched brings on a state of loneliness.  Katy needed to encounter the reality of Brian going; life doesn't go on in the same way.

For two days I allowed her to breathe; if she asked for affection then I gave it to her, and when she seemed expressionless and wanted time to think, I retreated to the caravan or busied myself someplace else.  Don't get me wrong, Katy was overjoyed that she's found the strength to send Brian packing.  Deep down she'd always known he was a sleaze bag and not a husband she'd trust in the company of women.  She admitted that his 'immediate' withdrawal from the Golf Club gang-bang was a lie from the start, and when he viewed the film over and over, she felt sure he'd had a piece of me.  I couldn't argue, there were so many dabblers that I didn't know who'd abused me.

Within two days of Brian leaving Katy got a job doing accounts at home on a computer.  She said she'd still pay the fifty pounds weekly rent for the caravan and dropped a hint that in a month or two she may let me move in with her.  I guess she has her daughters to think of – mummy in the same bed as Aunty Rosa, wearing no pajamas!

I suppose another change during these two days was my dithering allegiances.  Since my return there'd been no question that Tracey Cummings is everything I want from life; she is beautiful, exceedingly loving when she chooses to be, vulnerable when she's not faking a persona and is without a doubt a magician when it comes to sex.  Before a few days ago give me ten choices of who I'd love to be marooned on a desert island with, and TC would have got 10 votes.

What tops an allegiance with a sister, especially a sister like Katy?  We've grown close, and I'm not saying just how close because there are some things society doesn't approve of.  Right now Katy is my priority; that's not to say I would refuse several helpings of Sally's pale-pink body or abandon Marty to a life of celibacy, or turn down any offers of sex that come along, be it with the brothers, Harry, or in my wildest dreams, the ultimate sex goddess Tracey Cummings.  What I'm saying, is today at least, I and Katy are inseparable.


**Homage to Caroline**


A question my parents would doubtlessly ask if they knew all the details of my sexual adventures from last year and the present time is, am I trying to convert Katy into another version of me? They'd think I set out to ruin Katy's life, make her wear the 'Whore' badge on her lapel and become an outcast in this part of the city.  They'd tell Katy that her younger sister is a bitch, an unworthy bitch who's only happy when there's something between her legs.  Well, that's not true at all.  What I want for

Katy is to experience another side of life; there is more to a girl's existence than being a mother and preparing salads for her man's dinner.  Those girls who have missed out on the joys of sex have lost their innate sense of what's natural.  Look at all the female wild animals that are looking to be screwed by the alpha male – they hate missing out.  All I'm trying to do is introduce Katy to a world of pleasure, a world where neither she nor I had dipped our toes until a year ago.  If she doesn't wish to go on the journey, she's at liberty to tell me.

In a moment of togetherness, I ask her what she thought about the brothers – was it a one-off, or is she open to further adventures.  She's not beaming with enthusiasm, but places her hands on my cheeks and says, 'Rosa, depends on what you've got in mind.'

I suggest we go walking and contemplate taking her to the riverbank, maybe along the way I'll think of something better.  First, though, she wants to inspect the spot in the park where Brian raped me.  I don't ask why, maybe she's going to bury her memories in the glade, stamp down the earth and rid herself of Brian.  When we get there, she finds a streak of confidence and says, 'You were once so timid and naïve, Rosa... look at you now, even here you're unflustered.  You've gained toughness from doing what you do.  I'm not averse to doing something else.'

I pinch her bottom to halt the seriousness, joke that I know where there's a horse in a field, and she jokes back, 'If it's a pony...'

We come out of the park and take the road that leads to the street where Marty lives.  I'm making up all kinds of ludicrous ideas; we could go door-knocking, ask folks if they'd like our bodies for free, look out for workmen, maybe flag down a police car and have sex to a siren and a blue flashing light.  'Is that what you used to do?' Rosa says half-thinking it's true.  And as we're walking down my old street, I notice Marty's car; I slow down, tap Katy's shoulder and propose that we call for a coffee.

A couple of years back, Katy had a soft spot for Marty; he's a complete contrast to Brian although maybe that's not obvious after the description of his violent assault on my body. Katy says that she doesn't mind.  I knock on his door and enter, tell him that I've brought a surprise visitor.

Marty is polite; he thinks Katy is rather posh.  He asks about her children but he doesn't mention Brian.  The atmosphere over the next half-hour is cordial but the longer we sit there the more thoughts pop into my head.  And it's obvious what kind of thoughts rush through this brain of mine.  Dare I ask a question?  Dare I risk insulting either Katy or Marty?  'Hey, Marty,' I say.

'Yes, my still-on-speaking-terms-ex,' he says which is his attempt at humor.

'Mind if I show Katy my old bedroom?  I've told her about my mirrors – I'd like her to see them.'

'Feel free,' he says.  I'm sure Katy gets an inkling I'm being devious, but she follows me to the stairs and jabs her finger in my ass.

'Rosa...' she whispers.

'Don't panic, girl,' I say.  'If he can take Caroline up here, then I'm sure I can take you.'  On the landing, I show her indents on the railing from cable-ties.  I explain to her that Marty once wanted a threesome with Caroline – I found her repulsive and wouldn't join in.  I show her my mirrors.  Then I pull open one of the drawers in the white chest and show her Marty's straps.  She gasps as if she didn't know that folks used them in real life, well, not ordinary people anyway.

I tell her she'd look fabulous laid naked on the bed with her hands bound behind her back.  She could see her reflection and fantasize about being screwed.  'That's all you think about,' she laughs.

'You daren't do it,' I say.

'I know what you'll do,' says Katy.

'Promise, I'll sit on the side of the bed and look at you, no more.'

'It's Marty's house.'

'He wouldn't dream of coming upstairs unless I told him to.'

'Don't be crazy.'

'You're a chicken – I thought you were looking for different experiences.'

'It's not much of an experience laying on a bed,' she says.

'You don't know until you've tried it.  Being immobilized feels sensational.'

I can see she is saying yes and no to herself.  Then she looks me in the eye.  'If I do this, you're not going to… And Marty won't suddenly run upstairs…'

'Not without permission,' I say.  'Try it.  It'll be a laugh.'

'Shut the door.  If I don't like it you must release me immediately.  Deal?'

'It's a deal.'

I help Katy undress, and boy am I getting horny.  I act like we are two girls having fun.  I rush because I think maybe she'll chicken out.  Barely a minute passes before I got her hands bound behind her back and I laid her in the middle of my former bed with her head resting on two pillows.  I tell Katy to glance in the mirrors, then after she's approved, I tell her that it feels even better when there's a blindfold covering the eyes.  She allows me to blindfold her.  I reassure her that I won't touch her.  'Relax, enjoy the moment,' I say before I pretend to need a pee and inform her that I'll be back in a few seconds.  'Marty won't come upstairs unless I tell him to.'

As quietly as possible I race downstairs, asks Marty if he's any little blue pills.  He shows me one, I make him swallow it, then start to strip him.  He asks what's going on.  I whisper a description of the time that he brought Caroline here.  'You wanted me to do things with her... it's payback time... you're going to screw my sister... she's waiting for you.'

He gulps.  I encourage him to get horny.  I hear a muffled yelp from upstairs.  I lead Marty to the bedroom and tell Katy that I'm back.  'Is it nice, girl?' I say.

She speaks but I can't tell what she says.  I sit on the mattress and begin stroking her hair.  Oh, for five or six minutes I just keep on telling her to imagine what it would be like laying there with a big dick inside her.  It takes her a while to nod, and when she does, I summon Marty from the doorway and whisper in Katy's ear, 'You're getting one.'

I think Marty is more scared than Katy.  I have to urge him to get on the bed and do his damnedest.  It's me who gets up and parts Katy's legs and it's me who has to reiterate the promise that I won't abuse her.

Oh, what a moment – the man that I once love begins to screw my lovely sister who at first stiffens but quickly accepts that she's been outsmarted.  As he gets harder, her hips start to respond.  I tell her it is only Marty.  I stroke her hair, plant a few kisses on her breasts and signal to Marty to dig deep and give Katy some pleasure.  It is fabulous.  I feel I've achieved something. Sure, I'd love to dive in and have Katy for myself but a promise is a promise.  Those pills work beautifully and the sex goes on for ages.  Katy lets herself go and she even tries to lock Marty with her legs while I'm doing my best to keep my clothes on.  Yes, I succeed.  Yes, it's a glorious occasion, and when it's over there isn't a single complaint, not even from Marty.


**Post Marty/Katy blues**

I'm crazy.  I brought Katy a bunch of happiness.  She even commended me on my creative thinking and said she didn't have a clue what I had in store for her.  Oh, there was a touch of embarrassment about Marty, but as I and he aren't a couple anymore, she overlooked the former -brother-in-law status and concentrated on the pleasure and having gained another valuable sexual experience.  Katy treated me affectionately, let me sleep at her house for a second time and through many hours I was emotionally content.

It's only today that the rot's set in.  All morning I've been arguing with myself because I see myself as an instigator of good deeds for others and that's contrary to what I longed for when this process started.  Rosa Saint John used to be a shy withdrawn girl, always dominated by those around her.  I kind of hated her because I wanted to be dominated sexually, but not thought of as a doormat.

In the beginning, when I first got to know Tracey, she treated me like a slut.  Being a sex slave is adorable, and of course, we progressed through adventures and everything was hunky-dory until we fell in love.  I suppose if someone had taken me on and kept me in a cupboard, only letting me see daylight when they needed satisfaction, I'd still be relatively happy.  But that's not how it's worked out.  I'm feeling disappointed and this morning I just crave to be that girl who got accosted by Tracey Cummings on the lane behind the church.

Since my return, I can't think of an instance when anyone's chosen to overwhelm me (and don't go thinking Marty did during that vicious session in which he punched me; being rough was my idea; giving him free rein was my idea) and blatantly use me for his/her satisfaction. Those brothers have got it right. The crowd at the Golf Club had it right. And Tracey had it right. But somehow this morning I'm resenting Katy and having bad thoughts about Sally and Marty too. I'm giving these last three the privilege of pleasure but none of them asks me, or more precisely, tells me that I'm going to be stuffed senseless and I'll have no say in what's going to happen. I had no say with Brian, but that didn't last long enough to be classified as a sexual experience.

Am I being unfair? Is selfishness getting the better of me? All last year I felt superfluous to all needs but those of Tracey Cummings. Her only crime was to fall in love. But this year, or recently it's not superfluity that I feel, it's partial absolution, as if some folks are forgiving me for past sins but requiring me to be a sinner on their terms. 'You can lick me all you like,' yells Sally. 'If you think of it, I'll do it,' yells Marty. 'If I like the experience, which I won't know until after the event, I'll allow you to dream up more,' yells Katy. Wouldn't it be nice to be woken in the middle of the night, kidnapped by a gang of hunky young men, and get treated like the whore of all whores? Don't the folks who I'm having sex with ever think of inquiring what would Rosa Saint John like more than anything in the world – and the answer to that, this morning, is a second gang-bang. I call Tracey, and again she doesn't respond. I think asking Katy to join me in a gang-bang would be a step too far.

And that's not all if I'm totally honest.  All the input in sex sessions is mine.  I should place a notice in the shop window advertising for imaginative thinkers to get in touch.  I don't want to discuss their ideas on sex, I want to experience those ideas in practice.  Right now, I'd volunteer to be the guinea pig in sadistic experiments.  Fuck you, world!  This morning, that's how I'm feeling.


**No prizes for me… not yet…**

Hey, apologies for the outburst, I don't usually moan.  We all have off days, or off-mornings as is the case here.  I've just called at Katy's and she tells me that Brian has gone home to his parents in Scotland.  She received the news from a woman she communicates with on the internet.  I hope he gets swallowed by the Loch Ness Monster; he's no more the biggest bastard in England.


**Frustration unleashed**

One thing I've made clear from the start in my journal of 'The Life and Times of Rosa Saint John' is that I'm going to be as forthright as honesty can allow.  Yes, I've censored some happenings with Katy, but what follows is an accurate account of what can happen when a girl gets over-frustrated, when a girl is needing something that no-one accessible is giving her at eight o'clock in the evening. As I've said, had Tracey answered my calls, I wouldn't have had to resort to other measures.  If you don't wish to know what I've done, move on to the next heading.

Here goes…

I'm minding my own business, getting settled for a few hours of self-abuse. I've had a bit of alcohol though I'm not drunk – a little merry perhaps, but well capable of touching my toes without falling sideways. It doesn't take a professor to deduce that I'm in my underwear and recalling depraved scenes from my past in my head. Even with self-pleasure, you need to create an ambiance.

I'm sitting on the arced sofa when I hear a car pull to a halt. Harry and Sally have visitors, and from their voices, they appear to be middle-aged. I go to the caravan's rear window and attempt to snoop. There is mumbling after the visitors have knocked on the door but it's indecipherable. I wait. Five minutes later Sally comes from her door wearing a coat and she's accompanied by the folks who I assume are her parents. They pile into the parents' car; the car is driven off. And guessing the next bit is easy too. Instantly, I think that a lonely young man has been left alone in a big house. Yes, a big house that's cold and lonely without a woman. Should I say a lonely boy, or is that indecent? Anyhow, it takes me the best part of three seconds to plan what to do next. As shameless as I've been at any time in my past, I open the caravan door, go straight to the young couple's door in my underwear, and when Harry stands gazing in shock, I say, 'Is everything okay?'

'Yes,' he says attempting to keep his eyes fixed on my face instead of two other places.

'Sally doesn't usually go out,' I add.

His eyes fall to my tits. 'She's… er, er, gone to see her grandmother in the hospital,' says Harry.

'Oh,' I say. I alter my stance by putting the weight on one leg, slightly part one leg from the other, and of course, the poor boy's eyes drop further.  I will myself to net him.  I look at his crotch so he notices where I'm staring.

'How long will she be out?' I say.

He's trying so hard to lift his eyes to my face that he doesn't hear me.  'What?'

'How long will she be?'

'Two or three hours, I guess.'

And here comes the hook… I lower one side of my knickers by about two inches.  I pause, then say, 'How old is Sally?'

'Just gone eighteen,' he says quietly.

Ever so sexily I dip the other side of my knickers, move a few inches closer and whisper, 'Have you ever had a fully grown woman?'

'Not really,' he replies.  Not really - what kind of an answer is that.

I keep flicking my waistband, and very soon I'm flicking it so hard that my knickers drop down my legs.  He can't resist looking.  I tell him that I don't mind him looking but I'd prefer him to do more than that.  I bend down, pick up my knickers and turn to show him my ass.  'You've got five minutes before I lock my door.  I'll be sitting on my sofa waiting for you.  Show me what you can do – I'm fucking horny, and you're the guy to cure me.'

I walk away, and as soon as I get inside the caravan, I take off my bra and sit open-legged on the sofa.  I'm confident he'll come, but in my head, I say a prayer just in case I'm wrong.

Three minutes later Harry has his jeans low on his ass and he's pounding inside me like he's a train to catch in four minutes. I lean forward just once to pull off his shirt.  I encourage him, tell him I can take anything he has to offer.  But Harry's sex is plain and simple, ramrodding in, ramrodding out, blasting as if ejaculation is the sole object of screwing.  I keep pulling away to make it last, but he's in me again, out again, and it becomes a battle of wills.  I get my back flat on the cushions and he's pumping like a cleaner of drains.  Bang! Bang!  Hell!  Does a real woman enjoy being screwed by a boy/man?  She does, she does, but it should have endured for much longer.  Harry goes bright red, nods like he probably does at a supermarket checkout.  He grabs his shirt and leaves.


**Too much introspection**


The Rosa Saint John from a year back was like one of those folks on the high street who others perhaps recognize much like they do the white or yellow road markings.  There goes that uncomplicated girl who lives with that uncomplicated guy, Marty, in an uncomplicated three-bedroom semi.  Big Deal.  And I've got to say, apart from an attraction to sex, nothing much changed until recently, until mood swings came along.  This past week especially I've become angry with myself for no apparent reason.

Oh, some folks may accuse me of harboring guilt because I lured a young girl to the caravan and showed her what it's like to feel female.  And I lured her other half to my caravan and showed him what it's like to screw a body that moves.  There is no way I feel guilty.  I did both a favor and who knows how many more favors are yet to come.

And I've started to think that most of what I've done for Katy is favors.  Me showing her attention, being partly responsible for getting rid of Brian, introducing her to Kev and Timmy, allowing Marty to ravage her body while her wrists were strapped behind her back.  And how am I repaid?  I can tell you that I feel sore, kind of abandoned.  And don't go telling me that Katy has two daughters and she can't be a freeloader like me... I know, I know.  But since she started that accountancy job by plonking on a keyboard eight or nine hours a day, I think she's not interested in me anymore.  I'm not completely forsaken, but the odd kiss and cuddle, the ten-minute chats over coffee aren't exactly stirring my blood or satisfying my needs.  I've to ask her to show a bit of tenderness, I've to ask for... well, I've to ask.  I'm getting sick of being the chaser and as I've mentioned before it would be nice for someone/a whole gang of people, to come chasing me.  Rosa, get running because when we catch you, we're going to do unimaginable things to your body and when we've finished with you, you're going to be like a blow-up doll with its air sucked out.

Please, anyone who's listening, don't send requests, just take it without asking.

Three more phone calls to Tracey Cummings – nothing.

One text message from Marty reads, 'Come see me, around six, if that's okay by you.'

Katy lets me use her shower.  I scream from the landing for her to come to find the soap.  It doesn't add up (that's an accountancy joke) why she won't leave the keyboard.


## Is Marty for real?


Sometimes I think men's brains have the constitution of a pickled onion; between the folds, they don't have blood cells, and that what's in a female brain, but they have minute rivers of vinegar that warp their thinking processes.  I go to Marty's and immediately get bombarded with words of appreciation.  Oh, Rosa, what a sweet, sweet girl you are for bringing your sister here and taking her to OUR bedroom.  To strip her naked like that, to restrain her by the wrists so I could use up my little blue pill extra-plus energy on her lithe womanly curves and see you sitting calmly at her side while she enjoyed my machinery… Oh, Rosa, thank you, thank you, you are so kind and thoughtful. Few ex-partners in the universe would do such a splendid thing. You did it for me. You deserve sainthood. I can't express such fabulous generosity. YOU DID IT FOR ME!

Should I tell him that I did it for Katy? We sit in the armchairs and for once in his life he finds a way to wear an everlasting smile. He talks about the past, recalls the early days when we moved in together, talks obliquely about sex as if we were proper lovers but in reality, we screwed with our clothes on and in the dark. He paints a picture of happiness that's as interpretable as a Picasso, and he mentions days out as though they were Caribbean cruises that lasted for a month.

After an hour I start to wonder where this is leading, and to my surprise, it leads to the kitchen where he's prepared two plates of salad with a bottle of sparkling wine in the table's center. Marty repents his sins. He should never have been dazzled by Caroline's gift of a few paperclips and he shouldn't have screwed her ass on the office desk after his colleagues had gone home. He should never have expected for me to find a threesome with a huge black bush (aka hedgehog) irresistible, and as for Caroline filming me coated in tomato sauce and being humped from behind, he's sorry about that too. He can understand why I took Tracey Cummings to our bedroom and left the bed looking like a scene from a ten-woman orgy.

Oh, as it's time for confessions, I decide to offer a spoonful or two. 'What I and Tracey Cummings did could fill more editions than the Encyclopedia Britannica. I got two hundred quid from a rich American by laying naked on his hotel bed and letting him finger me.  I had a double dose of dick from two brothers on the council estate.  I was gang-banged by three trillion members of a Golf Club.  Almost screwed at a bus shelter in town.  And that doesn't include all the times I tried to get Vini's knickers off.  Yes Marty, and since I've come back, I've been raped in a park, eaten a young girl's pussy, taken a swift hammering from her young husband, and been more than a little naughty with my sister.'

He laughs, shakes his head, 'No…'

He didn't believe me before when I told him about the gang-bang during a row, and he doesn't believe a word of what I'm telling him.

'And I sat naked on old Geoff's lap.  And lapped-up my own company more than any girl would judge to be decent.'

He points to the salad and pours me a glass of wine then reiterates how happy we once were and just knows beyond any doubt that I brought Katy here to please him.  Last shakes of the dice… 'Do you know there's a film of me and Tracey at the Golf Club – mother and father have seen it.  They think I'm the dirtiest whore in history.'

Marty's smile drops for the first time.  Again, he shakes his head and his hand dives across the table to grab mine.  'You will do anything to put me off you.  I've said I'm sorry about Caroline.  I want to make amends.'

'Invite all the guys in the street to our bedroom to give me a good pummeling,' I say.

'Rosa, will you marry me, please…?'

Oh God, gift Marty a single brain cell.  May the Lord have mercy on his soul.

I get up, put the plates of half-eaten salad and the glasses of wine near the sink.  I take my clothes off and recline on the table.  'Do it, do it now,' I say.  'I'm responding in the only way I know how… I'm a fucking sex freak.  I'll let you screw me, but Marty, right now I don't want to be owned.'

'Will you move in with me?' he says.

'Let's wait.  Let's see what happens.'


**Triple let down**

I call at Katy's house on my way home; the kids are in bed and I hope Katy is in a mood to soothe my woes.  She's in her bathrobe, looks freshly showered, and smells like a perfume counter.  She keeps an arm's length between us.  I followed her from the kitchen to the room and back again.  She's not cold or particularly reserved but I'd like her to embrace me and say, 'What's wrong, sis?'

The fourth time I move in on her she does allow me to squeeze her waist and makes a joke about my hands wandering.  I rest my head on her shoulder and slowly release the news about Marty's proposal of marriage.  She acts surprised, and it could be me but I think she is wondering why anyone would want me as a wife.  She doesn't know all that I do but she's aware that I'm forever talking about sex like it's the one thing in life that I can't live without.

'It didn't work the first time,' she says.

'He cheated on me,' I say defensively.

'And haven't you cheated on him?' she responds.

She finds an excuse to look in a cupboard.  I make a remark about warming the caravan because it chilly tonight, and in a flash, she says, 'Oh, I'll see you later.'  There's not only me who's being temperamental lately.

Instead of going up the street, my feet carry me to the off-license where I buy a bottle of gin with one of my last twenty pound notes.  Then I almost run home with the cold air making my eyes watery and I get to believe that I'm crying inside.  Stupid, I know, but my spirits are crushed.  I exaggerate Katy's rejection.  I curse Marty for being a fool.  I scream inside because Tracey Cummings seems to be deliberately distancing herself.  I feel alone and angry and I just want to sob like a baby with a wet nappy.

Self-pity is a miserable emotion and I slam the door to warn the world that I don't need disturbing.  I and the bottle of gin are getting down to business.  I'm going to get naked, turn the small mirror on the cupboard door toward the arced sofa and watch a semi-retired whore get drunk.  Nobody wants me for a plaything so I'm better off inebriated and in a world of haziness where nothing in the mind is too serious.

Rosa watches me.  I watch Rosa.  Rosa the dirty bitch who even gets off on viewing her body.  She keeps pouring and gulping, pouring and gulping, sitting up to admire herself, standing up and wishing she were able to recline on somebody's lap.  I go from being angry to incorporating minutes of silliness.  I talk to myself, speak to Tracey Cummings like we're in the middle of a sex scene.  Yes, I go through the whole caboodle of what we used to do and wish I possessed all the toys in her top two drawers.  Then self-loathing comes, anger comes again and when the bottle is almost drained I start bounding around the caravan's interior yelling, 'Screw me, will some fucker screw me,' and I'm out of control and don't give a damn if men carrying a straight-jacket burst through the door.

I fall against the units, stagger to my feet only to fall again, to curse some more and to be rowdy as I can be.  Take me to a torture chamber and give me something pleasant to think about.  Then I fall close to the doorway, start muttering obscenities when the door presses on my feet and I hear voices asking, 'Rosa, are you okay?  Rosa, is that you?'

'Who the fuck it that?'

Harry and Sally make their way into the caravan.  I gaze up at them.  'Well, well...'  Then I put one leg in the air and rest my foot on a padded edge, stretch my other leg as far as possible from the other, grab my tits and squeeze them.  'Who's for an orgy?' I say joyfully.

They glare at each other and even though I'm wonderfully drunk I know that each is fearing that I'll reveal that I've had sex with both of them.  Sally reacts first, she runs a flannel under the taps and crouches over me, mopping my brow, pretending to be a nurse and telling me to raise my head.  Harry is frozen on the spot.  I want to yell that I've been to places on his young wife's body where he wouldn't dream of going.  Then I tell Sally that she's a fine specimen of girlhood.  'Let's all have sex,' I say.  'I'm not choosy – this end or that end – let's make a night of it.'

They're decidedly nervous, especially Sally who doesn't stop fussing and asking me inane questions such as, 'Have you been drinking?'

I tell them to screw me on the floor, take me to bed, screw me on the sofa.  I feel so empty.  I need attention.

Sally's only weapon is to drown out my voice.  Harry's weapon relies on luck – the luck that I'll withhold the knife that is capable of destroying them.  They both lift me, assist me to my bed, then Sally forces a wet cloth in my hand and tells me they're going, go to sleep, I'll feel better in the morning, we all get down at times – go look for a dog in the street to screw!  She says anything that will escort her feet to the caravan doorway and make good their escape.  They leave, and I praise myself for being a Christian and not exposing their secret misdemeanors.


**Consequences and a surprise reunion**

A thick-headed morning and a fruitless afternoon walking the streets of the council estate leave me feeling dejected.  I even passed the gateway to my parents' house and stuttered on the curb.  Who is left in this world who will welcome me?  Which kind person desires to bind me to their bedposts and feast on a body that's keen to be eaten?  Only Marty… good old Marty who's repentant for his sins with Caroline and her hedgehog.  Good old Marty who's only noteworthy idea was to purchase little blue pills, but then they may have been recommended by his boss.  I can hear Marty uttering, 'What do you mean by eat you?'  I can see Marty calling a hot-line and asking for advice.  Dejection is something dripped on you by others.

After Katy's recent reluctance to cavort with her sister while her daughters have been at school, I'm disinclined to call. She may stand two arm's lengths away, be dressed in an Anderson shelter with sandbags protecting her access points, she may accuse me of shattering her marriage and blame her adventures with the brothers and dear old Marty on my desire to own a harlot sister.  So easy, Katy could return me to the outcast club – 'I want you only as a sister at the end of a phone whom I can nuclearize with tales of my brilliant girls.'  In life, one arm's length can rapidly become a mile and a mile can become a silence such as the one existing between me and Tracey Cummings.

Be brave, ye girl of immense longings, tap on her solid wood door and pray for the glimmer of a smile.

'Why didn't you just enter?' says Katy shocked by a knock and the gray deadness of my expression.

'I thought...'

'Don't be silly.  I love you, you're my best friend.'  She permits me entry so long as I leave desolation on the doorstep.

Katy is loving.  Katy is big-sisterly.  Katy puts her warm arm around my shoulder and says, 'Oh, love, I've seen Sally.  She tells me that her parents need to retrieve the caravan so they can take grandmother on holiday.  They're coming for it tomorrow.'

They – the happy couple – forfeit fifty pounds a week rent and my generous invitation of a lovefest in a cramped space.  Holiday for granny, my ass!  After the thrills I've given them, especially those sent to Sally's beautiful sweet-tasting organ.  Shit!

'Oh, gosh,' I say innocently, 'it looks like I'm homeless.'

'Would I see you out on the streets?' says Katy.  'Go collect your things and put the key through the letterbox.  We'll have a girlie chat when you come back.'

I now know how it must feel for women who begin a diet and vow to ditch cream buns and their favorite delights.  Nevermore... nevermore to sink my lips in that cute arena of fabulous form.  Nevermore to give birth to a dream when Harry rides off on his motorbike.  When I collect my possessions, I touch the seat where she sat and regret I had her but twice.

Until late in the evening Katy and I spoke of love.  Sure, it was an odd conversation, as both of us were spitting out thoughts but not communicating.  Katy said there'd always been something left in reserve when she and Brian got together; as if she didn't wholly trust him, as if he'd a side to his character that she'd never encountered.  How right she'd been.  Biggest bastard in Scotland now.

As for me, I told Katy that I and Marty were conveniences for each other.  We wandered into a relationship because neither of us had choices.  Much of the time we were like siblings, sharing odd interests but going about separate lives without that spark of togetherness.  I surprised myself when I mentioned Josivini (Vini), my café workmate, but as I say we were rambling, unhindered by worrying what each other thought.  I explained I'd had a mighty crush on the Fijian girl and I once took her to the riverbank in the hope of seducing her.  Vini had a super body, better than mine, better than most women on the planet.  But what I didn't say perhaps would have been the most revealing.  I didn't tell Katy about Tracey Cummings.  And the big difference between TC and just about everyone else in my life is that TC loved me big style.  She craved for my company, yearned for my body, said occasionally that she couldn't live without me.  Being loved makes a girl want to love in return.  Being wanted and desired gets the mind going to places it's never been.  I think, apart from Katy, Tracey Cummings is the one person who's loved me unreservedly.  Of course, her downfall was that she couldn't bear love's excruciating pain.

So where does this leave us, me and Katy?  In love more than is natural for sisters.  It's true to say that I desire her, and she desires me but can't escape the boundary of what is socially acceptable.  She's constantly aware she's an example to set for her daughters.  She fears ostracism by our parents.  And maybe she believes I'm too much of a risk.  Once a girl's been gang-banged she's destined for a life of corruption.

That evening we loved each other; cuddled, kissed, sort of mild embraces that weren't particularly sexual.  We went to bed late, but when I awoke in the morning Katy was already rattling on

her keyboard.  I instantly had the notion that I'm third in line
behind her girls and her employment.


**Chance encounter**

I hang on.  I hang on with a smidgen of hope that a new day
shines a new light on my thoughts.  I hang on urging Katy to take
to a wine bottle where any inhibitions may drown and be flushed
from her body.  Surely a lifetime of happiness supersedes a cupful
of reservations!

The second new day I go for a walk up the street toward
the park; nothing is bothering me; my head is blank and I'm
enjoying the early summer sunshine.  Not too far from the park,
there is a walled corner where two streets meet.  I turn the corner
and almost collide with a body turning close to the wall.  For a
second, I and the body are inches apart; it's a smaller body that
belongs to a face I recognize.  The mouth of the face drops open.
'It wasn't my idea,' she says.

'Sally...'

'Harry said we should get rid of the caravan.'

I run my eyes over her front.  I can tell that she'll just
stand there and listen to anything I say.  'If there weren't so many
folks about, I'd take you to the park...'

'Would you,' she says shyly.

'And do you know what I'd do to you?'

Maybe she thinks I'd beat her up.  Her eyes fall.  'What?'
she asks fearfully.

'Exactly what I did to you before.  You are gorgeous.  I
never stop picturing you naked.  When can we have sex?'

She swallows nervously.  I tell her to put my number in
her phone.  I tell her that next time I have her she'll realize that
Harry is a little boy.  I'll give her so many orgasms she'll want me
between her legs for eternity.  She shakes, even places one hand
on her crotch but looks immensely scared.  She receives my
number then tells me she's got to go.

'Call me,' I say.  'I'll take you somewhere.  Remember, I
keep my promises.'

She waves childishly.  Maybe not everything is lost.


**The ease of letting go**

When Katy informs me that she must put in a ten-hour shift on
the keyboard I sulk on her sofa like a punished toddler.  No fun
today.  I foresee us going to bed at midnight, her falling asleep as
soon as her head hits the pillows and me spending the hours of
darkness wondering whether to run to the red light district and
offer myself for free.

I find the nerve to ask Katy in a roundabout way if she'd
be offended if I spend a night or two at Marty's – 'Oh, no Katy,
I've no intention of renewing our relationship, I just thought... I
just thought that you seem to have a lot of work to catch up on
and I'll be a distraction... making coffee, going in and out...
bouncing on the shower basin as I amuse myself.'

Katy gives me a stunner full on the lips, combs my hair
with her fingers and says happily, 'Yes, you do, girl, I'll give you a
change of scenery.'

Why didn't she drag me upstairs after pleading she can't
do without me?  Why the ease?  Why not say I'm allowed out for
an hour but I want you back here at 4, 5, 6, or even half-past?  I

collect most of my things (I've hardly got a caseload), blow Katy several kisses then set off down the road.  Then I call Marty.  He can be home in ten minutes.  'We need to talk,' I say.

'What about?'

'Tell you when I get there.'

When Marty sees the bag, he assumes I'm going to accept his proposal of marriage.  We arrive at the same time and he unlocks the door as if our honeymoon is about to commence.  He stands aside, lets me pass him, slaps my ass and says how good it is to see me.  He's so relieved; he thought I'd be in touch.  Are his pockets loaded with little blue pills?

'Look, Marty, it's not how it seems...'

'I wasn't judging,' he says.

'What about if I spend a few nights here... no strings attached... no threesomes with girls I disapprove of... I'm not telling you that you can't have other women if you don't tell me I can't have other...'  I was going to say girls but at the last seconds said 'men'.

'So, it's not just me and you,' he says fractionally, only fractionally disappointed.

'Who knows what will happen, but I feel it's fair to make it clear that I'm not living under restrictions.  To be perfectly honest, I'm broke.  I need you to keep me.  I'll sleep in our bed and I'm not going to wear a chastity belt.  Is that reasonable?'

'I suppose,' he says as I lift my skirt to scratch an itch.

Wow!  I catch him staring like he's been missing me.  I purposely raise my skirt higher and he doesn't avert his eyes.  I think about tormenting him, then decide to hoist my top over my belly.  He shuffles on his feet.  'Are you hungry,' I say.

I walk backward to the edge of the sofa, release my skirt and let it fall, then I point both arms directly upward and invite him to remove my top.  Sure, it's me leading as usual but God, it's been a million years since I last had sex.  I lay with my back on the sofa cushion and for once Marty does what's required without dipping in his pocket for a little blue pill.  'Welcome home,' he says when I'm smiling moderately satisfied.

'Do those pills work after you've already been active,' I say.

'No idea,' he says, 'it's worth trying.'


**Unexpected bonuses**

I've got to say, after Marty returned to work, I pranced around the house in just my knickers and realized how good it felt to be back. This is the first time in not much short of a year that I've got sex on tap; sure, I'll regularly have to tell Marty what to do, but it's better than having to seize irregular opportunities for fulfillment. This is my place, what I used to call home – I can strip off, amuse myself, go out, have a shower, not worry about money, clean up if I desire, jump on our bed, sneak in a football team through the rear door, and generally be free to live on my whims.  So long as Marty doesn't harbor ideas of settling down to a life of domesticated bliss, just him and me, all will be fine and dandy.

It's also a shorter distance from here to Tracey's house. Maybe some of the girls I used to get on with will start talking to me and have clues as to what Tracey is doing with her life.  Maybe if I get super-horny, I can call at Geoff's and ask if the brothers know any variations to the black hood routine.  But don't go thinking I'm deserting my sister because presently she's the only one who reciprocates love, not in a physical sense, but she does love me, and it would be nice if that love isn't broken as it was after my starring role at the Golf Club.

I make Marty a decent dinner, not a boring salad, but potatoes, steak, peas, and thick onion gravy.  I get him to screw me as I lean on the bathroom wall, then again as he walks around the upstairs with my legs wrapped around his waist.  And when he goes to sleep, I start assembling ideas of who I'd choose for a threesome.  He had his turn with Caroline – surely, I can come up with a better companion than her?  But as ever, no matter what I dream-up or fantasize over, the longing to be roughly possessed never goes away.  It is in my nature to be dominated and while ever I'm luring others to me, I regret that they are not affording me the same privilege.


**An interesting development**

Reading about celebrities leaves the impression that their lives are a constant stream of excitement.  Real-life is never fully exciting; between events there are periods of ordinariness – washing, eating, emptying the rubbish bin, scratching the ass, plucking the eye-brows, and a host of other tasks that are all unremarkable.  So, as with celebrities, don't think that I spend 24/7 on a sexual high.  Irrespective of how I come across, there are long stretches every day that are unremarkable, even boring.

An end-of-the-week day found me tapping my fingers Marty-style on the sofa arm.  I'd phoned Tracey to no avail.  I'd looked for a message from Sally.  I'd mused about heading to town on the bus.  I'd drunk four cups of coffee.  Boredom!

Seeing a dark-haired woman pass the window, I began to think about Katy.  Soon after, guilty thoughts arose in my head.  It had been several days; I'd neglected her apart from a couple of phone calls. I ask Marty if he is going out; he isn't. I decide that a trip to Katy's is overdue and leave the house within minutes.

I'm unsure of the reception I'll get; the day or two I'd left for had become almost a week. Broken promises are unwise for those hoping for developments and the more Katy's fingers glue to that keyboard the less time she'll reserve for me. I buy her some flowers on the way, get the kids a few nutrition bars and start thinking of excuses for not calling sooner. But just as I reach her house, she's stepping down the steps with her girls in tow.

I give her the flowers. She explains that the girls are going to our parents for the afternoon and then she thanks me. I can come along. 'I'm not welcome there,' I say.

'We won't stay, perhaps we can go for a walk?'

I agree, then Katy rushes back into her house and deposits the flowers. Through her front window, I see her squirt a little perfume on her neck and wrists. Maybe she's missed me. Maybe it's my lucky day.

On the journey to our parents' house, she says that she's caught up with her work and that it's quiet without me. I refer to sleeping alone. She smiles, adds nothing.

Anyhow, mother and father are hostile; they wince as I go through the doorway and I retreat to wait for Katy outside. Katy comes out, sweeps her hand across my hair and tells me she loves me. 'Let's go have fun,' she says.

'Fun?'

'Yes, where do you want to go?'

I get suspicious as I suggest several places that all get rejected. I tell her about the riverbank and how private it is down that hidden path, I've been naked, sunbathed, and listened to the water for hours. There's no-one to see us. We could be...

'What's Marty doing?' asks Katy out of the blue.

I'm sidetracked, feel kind of sickened because as I'm thinking what we could do on the riverbank she's bringing up the place I've just escaped from. 'He's...' I begin.

'Let's pop in. I'll say 'hello' then we'll take up one of your suggestions.'

It's only a two-minute walk so I don't object. I note that never before has Katy invited herself to my house. Maybe she's just being friendly, been without company, spent too much time on her keyboard. I'm surprised that she holds my hand as we walked down my street. She tells me that I look fabulous but I'm dressed in my usual skirt and top.

Marty remarks that I'm soon back home as I put my head through the doorway. His face lights up when he sees Katy. 'Hello, stranger,' he says before kissing her cheek. We sit, there's a lot less talk than I'd expected. Katy and Marty appear to be waiting for me to lead the conversation.

'It's an improvement on the last occasion I had two lovely girls in the house,' says Marty eventually. I remind him that Caroline wasn't a lovely girl and Katy has been here before.

It's impossible, I know, but I'm getting a feeling that they have set up this meeting; they keep on looking at me as if they're awaiting orders. Could there have been a secret phone call...?

Sure, I'm aware that my mind diverts to sexual activities the minute an opportunity arises and perhaps because I muse about the last time the three of us were here. Do I look for conspiracies that don't exist? The urge to bleat about my frustrations grows. There's a little talk about Katy and Marty's new jobs. Someone mentions 'other people' and I suggestively blurt, 'Who needs others, there's enough of us for a threesome.'

Well, at least I light their faces.  They feign jokey indignation and copy each other by murmuring 'What?'

'We all know it's going to happen,' I say casually.  I raise my hand, 'Volunteers?'

'Threesome?' questions Katy like she doesn't know what a threesome is.

'You, Marty.  Me, Marty.  You and me.  All three of us together,' I say to not allow the suggestion to wither in silence. 'No holding back, full-on filth,' I add.

'Don't know,'' whispers Marty as he glances at Katy.

I stand, think shit to it, if Katy hopes this is going to be like the last time when I was little more than a bystander, then she's wrong.  My sister is getting the full works, and I mean the full works.  I snatch her hand; she is easy to pull from the seat and towards the stairs; she keeps looking back to see if Marty is following but I tell her not to worry about him, he'll follow like a sheep.

God, it's amazing how quickly I turn myself on.  I'm lifting Katy's dress above her head by the time we reach the landing. She yelps, 'Rosa! Rosa!'  I'm taking no prisoners (wrong expression?).  This is what I've been waiting for since I first kissed her in her shower.  It's three-way sharing this time.

I'm sorry to disappoint, but I'm not going to detail what happened during the next hour, but I'll say this for starters... it doesn't appear to me that Marty needed his little blue pill.  The conclusion I draw from this is that to him, Katy's a turn-on – she's a sleek gorgeous piece of flesh that's a lot more pleasing to the eye than Caroline.  She's sexy too, and believe me, when her muscles go into overdrive, she lets herself go.  Well, on this occasion she let herself go and I'm not complaining.  However, I observed something that tells a story all of its own.

Marty is laid on his back with a giant erection. I'm kneeling at the end of the bed waiting for Katy to do what I think she'll do. But hey, Katy doesn't do what I think she'll do, instead, she goes crab-like and lowers herself on top of him, facing me, readying to dive in. I'm pleased, and yes, it got wonderfully erotic, but that's not the story.

This is the story... that's no action from a woman who's spent her married life in the missionary position. I can praise myself for educating her, I can praise myself for showing her possibilities of what the human body can do. But the way Katy so effortlessly performed that magic, the precision she showed by landing on her sweet spot, tells me that she and Marty have done that maneuver before, more than once. She was so confident that she grinned at me as my face fell forward. I became so unbelievably aroused knowing they were protecting secrets, and I made sure that Katy felt my wildness.

When I started this journey almost twelve months ago, I called myself Rosa Naivety Saint John, but now I'm not such a fool, not blind or gullible. I'm not in the slightest jealous, and I'm pleased that two folks I don't mind sharing with have more than a little in common, though what their ideas for the future are....?


**Words with former friends**

I cross paths with Belinda, Miranda, Sara, and Genni. At one time or another, each of them has blanked me since returning to Leeds. At first, they're cold and standoffish, and ask, 'What am I doing back – have I run out of men to sleep with in other parts of England?'

I laugh it off.  I used to feel inferior, be rather quiet in their company, but times have changed; no-one intimidates me anymore.  'I'm on the look-out for women now,' I say, but you're all safe – too old and ugly for my tastes.'

They think I'm joking and say I've acquired a sense of humor.  Am I back with Marty?  Am I rejoining the Fat Club?  If they go on a girls' night out, do I want to tag along?  I avoid their questions and when an opportunity arises, I mention Tracey Cummings; has anyone seen her around?

Belinda has seen her get on the bus, but as far as she understands Tracey spends much of her time elsewhere.  Women on the estate don't need to lock up their husbands and partners.  Maybe Tracey Cummings is a reformed character and has a job in a massage parlor – the massage parlor being Belinda's attempt at a joke.

Ten minutes of chatting, then I leave them to go to the Fat Club.  It's odd why they've not seen Tracey – who knows what's happened to her?


**Private thoughts**

Some thoughts are like bubbles in a simmering pan of soup – they keep on bubbling; you don't mind telling anyone about the soup but describing the bubbles is like exposing your soul.  The truth is that I'm not gloriously happy.  Don't get me wrong, having renewed my relationship with my sister, Katy, and making some kind of deal with Marty, as well as being financially secure again due to Marty's generosity, I shouldn't have too much to complain about.  And when I think about all those cold, lonely nights and the feelings of hunger and desperation I had during my exile on the South Coast, I ought to be yelling from the rooftops that Rosa Saint John has not had it so good for quite a period.

But as I say, in my pan of soup two bubbles swell and burst almost every hour of my existence.  I never stop recalling what it felt like to be loved by Tracey.  When someone wants you for who you are, when someone has the desire to spend every spare minute with you, can't get enough of you, adores you in every possible way, well, that gives a sensation of completeness, warms the heart, makes the body feel like it knows all its requirements will be fulfilled.  I remember that sense of worthiness – I wasn't an outcast; I had been claimed by a girl who loved me and if she'd have dared to suffer love's pain until she became used to being in love, well, we'd be together now, probably laying on her dirty pink sheet and dreaming up some yet unpracticed sex act.  It's not so much that I love Tracey Cummings that keeps me going, it's more that she loved me like no other had loved me before.  I doubt that I'll find that special connection again unless somehow, I'm fortunate and rediscover Tracey.  Yes, I go about my life being unable to share this feeling; I doubt there's a person in Leeds who'd go to the end of the earth to own the love of a whore, apart from me, that is.

And the other bubble… it's a giant bubble that swells not just in a pan of simmering soup but spreads throughout my body repeatedly.  I can walk the streets, be sleeping in bed, eating, cleaning, standing at a shop counter, talking to Marty or Katy when I get this overwhelming desire to be the victim of some appalling sex act.  As I've mentioned, to be utterly dominated is my unrivaled perfection.  That feeling of being the ultimate tart, getting treated how I deserve to be treated, being powerless, being exposed to unrestrained sex where there is no choice, there is no escape, there is only the fulfillment of others that will bring about freedom; it is that feeling that I long to experience again. Oh, I keep those sensations from the gang-bang in a special compartment in my head; they are incomparable with those from other sexual experiences – these sensations are different and complete the identity of Rosa Saint John like the last piece in a jigsaw complete a picture.  I understand that there'll be folks out there who find my thoughts incomprehensible – there must be something psychologically wrong with me.  I am a freak, I belong in the nut-house, I need therapy – all I can say to these folks is that the truth is immutable, and I'm not lying about my thoughts. I'd give anything to lay on that table again and have the crowd abuse me.

And recently… yes, I've never revealed this thought either… I've been thinking that Brian has gone to his parents in Scotland.  Brian, the guy who held his mobile phone that recorded the action of me and Tracey being superbly violated, is no longer visiting the Golf Club.  There won't be anyone to put on a film show for mother, father, and Katy, or even Marty if he's interested.  I've fantasized about going there one evening, just dawdling into that room filled with tables and chairs, standing on one table in the center and performing a striptease while the menfolk clear a space for me to be gang-banged.  Is that shocking?  I strongly believe that other women have crazy fantasies that are equally outrageous.  Show me a woman who hasn't thought of what sex different to what she is experiencing is like, and I'll show you a woman missing out on life's potential.  No woman has a goddam right to criticize girls who've had multiple sex partners at the same time because she doesn't know what thrills there are for the taking.  Those thrills leave an impression; all these months after the event and the impression is rich in my memory.

**We'll fly high in the sky**

With Marty at work, I take yet another walk to the council estate in the hope of unearthing clues to Tracey's whereabouts. I go there after calling at the precinct to establish if the café has re-opened – I'd had the silly notion of getting a part-time job just to meet some new folks or folks I know from working there before. The shutters remain down. I'm not disappointed. I'm disappointed after knocking harder on Tracey's door and receiving no response. Her neighbors haven't seen her for a week or more, but when I peep through her window, I see evidence that she still lives there. One day this will end, I think, one day I'll trap Tracey in a corner and she won't be so elusive.

I do a lap of my local area, pass my parents' house but don't call in, call in at the shop that banned me for returning a moldy loaf of bread – I get served; the couple that owns the shop must have forgotten my face.

Ten minutes later I'm heading toward Katy's wondering if she's added her numbers and can spare an hour for a spell of togetherness. I won't quiz her about what's going on with her and Marty; what goes on between the two of us is more important, especially because my mind is set on finding someone to screw before the day is out. The truth about raging hormones can be unpleasant to record.

I reach Katy's street from the lower end and think maybe I should have dressed more spectacularly, at least showed off my legs with a shorter skirt and perhaps sprayed myself with perfume. I pray her fingers aren't tapping her keyboard and muse that she'll be in the shower eager to welcome me and offer me more than a cup of coffee.

I'm met with a moment of serendipity a few yards from Katy's gate.  A figure a few houses higher up, leaves her garden and sets off in the direction of the park.  Oh God, my thighs go into overdrive – I never expected to see Sally in a summer outfit looking as sweet as a strawberry with a blob of cream.

I scamper past Katy's window, glance fleetingly to see if she's in her room.  I make it to the next house unseen and Sally is about thirty yards off, not looking back.

I tell myself that she's not called me – it is through fear or denial of another encounter?  Did she mean it when she said that it had been Harry who'd objected to my continuing stay in their caravan?  I must learn the truth.  If I can have her, I shall have her soon.

She enters the park gates.  I hang back; there are folks about who may be her neighbors.  Her pace slows and my heartbeat quickens – I've never done this before, and as I recall Brian's assault on me, I think I'm behaving no better than he did.  But as strong sunlight lashes on Sally's body and I see the outline of her ass through her skirt, I decided to catch her, to give her one last chance for us to have sex.  She reaches a bench, considers sitting but heads off toward the far gate.  I want her here, among the trees and the bushes.  I think about luring her from the eyes of strangers to a shielded spot unseen by everything but the heavens.

I call out her name.  She looks over her shoulder, freezes sideways on.  Her head droops.  I hurry toward her, 'You've not called me,' I say.

'I can't call you.'

'You dare not call me.'

'Harry would find out.'

'How?' I say.

She doesn't know; he'd just find out.  It would be the end of them.  She can't risk it.  'Please, leave me alone.'

I place her chin in my fingers.  'Tell me you don't want sex with me.'  She doesn't answer.  'Tell me that no-one has ever pleased you as I have pleased you.'

'They haven't,' she murmurs.

'Let me take you somewhere.  I promise you more than I have ever given you.'  She is deliberating but not obviously going to relent.

I think about taking her to Katy's.  Would Katy wish to share her?  Could Katy be so adventurous as to have a lesbian threesome?  Then I consider my feelings... sharing Sally is unthinkable, like offering half of a favorite cream bun.  I know the taste of her, I know how fabulously erotic it feels going down on her.

I point to the thicker area of woodland.  She shakes her head.  I mention her house.  'Out of bounds,' she says.  The riverbank.  Her parents travel along that road in their car.  I suggest we go to my house.  She is adamant; she won't go anywhere if there's the smallest chance of being discovered.

She hasn't once said that she won't have sex with me.  I tell her how beautiful she is, even go so far as to describe what I intend to do to her.  As the minutes pass, I watch her belly go inwards as if she's recalling past sensations; her fingers stretch like she's remembering me touching her.  I say more disgusting words until I feel certain that she is trapped in her desires, then I take her hand and lead her to the top end of the park to a place where I and Marty used to hide when we were courting.

She asks frequently where we are going.  I evade giving direct answers.  Oh, what I think of to say is like foreplay and we both know we are minutes from engaging in sex.

We reach the tower block where Marty lived as a teenager.  It has a security door, but I just wait for an occupant to leave before gaining entry.  I take Sally into the elevator and press the button for the ninth and top floor.  As we ascend, I kiss her, fondle the outside of her thighs and remind her we are seconds from bliss.  She remains silent, submissive; already she is trembling and bobbing her head like she's preparing to look at me directly.

On the ninth floor, there is a bolted door to the tower block roof.  There is a trick to undoing the bolt; a couple of sharp jerks, then tug it swiftly away from the hinge, and it opens.  I lead Sally by the hand to the roof; we can gaze over Leeds over the low surrounding wall and there is only the police helicopter, if passing, that will be able to see us.

She doesn't move unless I lead her.  She looks at me to declare that she's helpless in my hands.  There are protrusions on the roof all shapes and sizes.  I sit her on the edge of a large flat rectangle and ask if she's happy.

'I'm happy now,' she says offering me her hand.  I hold it, stare at her for some time and tell her that her body is her fortune; if I could spend a week screwing anyone, I'd choose her.  She seems flattered and her cheeks redden.  I ask her if she's ready and she nods gently.

Oh, ever so carefully, as if I'm parting the wings of a butterfly, I undress Sally and my eyes feast on the delights of her flesh.  I even take off her tiny white socks and lay them neatly at her side with the rest of her clothes.  This is going to be special; she's going to remember this day all her life.

With the most patience I've ever shown, I take Sally on a supreme marathon through all the heady degrees of intimate sex, building her sensations minute after minute, allowing her to melt a little before progressing to melt her some more.  It is 30 minutes before I penetrate her, over an hour before I taste her with my tongue, and I watch her lily-white skin tan in the brilliant sunshine and watch her lips thicken and darken in the heat of incredible bliss.  She's never climbed to such heights and gives me all I could ask for; she opens herself, lays out her arms to receive every single pleasure.  She glides through a constant orgasm that has no beginning and no end, and all the while I imagine that this will be the final contribution to my existence as a giver and the next stop on my adventure will be at the Golf Club.  This experience is among the sweetest, and perhaps for Sally, it shall never be matched.  Two hours after we came here, we leave and part with a soft kiss by the edge of the park.  I tell her there will be a next time.  I won't forget her.  Her amazing body is painted on my soul.  She doesn't realize that her socks are in my pocket as a trophy of success.


**Into reverse**

I vowed to rediscover that girl who I used to be – the one who submits, the one who is led to slaughter.  Those hours on top of the tower block were my final hours of giving and the transformation has begun.

Apart from Marty and Katy having clandestine sessions in her house or our house, the other major change came in two more threesomes.  Katy is getting the hang of it, Marty is getting used to it, and I'm altering my role in it.  That ideas person I'd become is reverting to her role as a victim.  During two threesomes I became lazier and lazier, refused to take the lead, refused to make suggestions and forced them into using me in a way they'd not done previously.  Maybe they thought I was moody or even wanting out.  I didn't care.  They can treat me as a victim or not at all.

And when our next threesome came, they'd conspired to tie me in Marty's straps, wrists to ankles, in a blindfold and gag; I just lay there helplessly, lapping up the punishment and feeling as good as at any time since my return.  I didn't compliment them but gave them the impression that they hadn't tried hard enough.  Katy isn't exactly a master like Tracey Cummings, but she promised improvements, and so did Marty.

Meanwhile, I'm thinking non-stop about visiting the Golf Club.  Surely, if the members didn't die last year of excitement, they're going to vote for a rerun despite there only being me.  Asking Katy to volunteer I'm sure is a step too far.  I've even put a note through Tracey's letterbox asking her to get in touch if she fancies going with me, and I've texted her.


**Another warm-up**

During one of Marty's mysterious disappearances, I call at Geoff's to ask if his boys will do me a favor.  Old Geoff says that Kev and Timmy are out.  He can guess what the favor is but he becomes cagey.  He has me standing in his kitchen like he's unsure as to what to do.  Geoff doesn't do anything out of hand but his mind is ticking and I think he's going to surprise me.  He goes into the hall and makes a phone call and when he returns, he tells me that the brothers should be here in the morning.  For some reason I don't believe him; he just laughs quietly and says, 'Get back across the field to where you came from.'

I leave, pause at the top of the cul-de-sac and wonder how Tracey was able to attract so many men without trying. Admittingly she'd go to pubs in town but she'd had plenty of guys from these parts – where are they now?

I start making my way across the field, all the while looking out for buses that may be transporting Tracey homeward. I give up when I near the path that leads behind the church and consider displaying my body on the sofa for when Marty gets home. As I get to the first stones on the path, I hear footsteps; someone is running and I look over my shoulder. There's a scramble, and in seconds I'm being lifted horizontally; I know Kev and Timmy have seized me and they're taking me to the woods. They laugh, and I feel my knickers being ripped off sideways. They're tossing me about and letting their hands roam on my body. 'Where's the black bag?' I say, but they're being rough and it's difficult to talk. They cart me up a small hill and into a clearing behind the sycamore trees.

Oh God, it's quick. My skirt is a belt around my waist and my top is folded over my head and my bra serves as a necktie. They put me doggy-position on the grass, merely undo the front of their pants then hammer into me in turn like a football match kicks off on television in a minute or two. It's Timmy then Kev. Twenty seconds each blasting me and calling me 'a fuck'. Timmy and Kev, Kev and Timmy using me as if I'm a rabbit, going hell for leather, bang, bang, squirt, squirt, 'That's what you wanted, girl – don't complain.' I fall forward flat on my face with my ass still up in the air. They slap my ass cheeks, tell me I'm lucky that they don't charge me, and then they run off home to the cul-de-sac.

I search for my knickers, can't find them, then just as last year, I have to walk home with semen running down my thighs. At least I get back before Marty. I shower, and in the nick of time am ready to receive him – 'Want to screw me?' I say when he walks through the door.  He screws me because he doesn't dare to refuse me.


**Don't judge me too harshly**

I do not doubt that there are folks out there in the big NORMAL world that will view me as a female from a different species.  If I'd been a mother, I'd be thinking of my kid all day and all night.  I am not a mother, so I think about sex.  I say in response to those who judge me as a freak, hold a mirror to your face – do you fuss over recipes? do you fret over housework? are you job-obsessive? Is your preoccupation with family? do you go from one day to the next always pondering about the same things?  Change your fixation to mine... there's no goddam difference; what drives one person doesn't drive another but, in the end, we're all humans with individual perversions and specific traits of character.  You can't be me and I can't be you.  You do what the hell you like and I'll do the same.  There's as much fundamental wrong with a sex maniac as there is with a girl who collects bangles; we put our hands through holes for satisfaction.  Big deal.

As I see it, at this moment, I've succeeded in getting partial absolution from what my critics would describe as my sins. There are one or two people who accept my idiosyncrasies and don't deny me the right to be an individual – praises to Marty, Katy, and Sally, and even to Kev and Timmy.

I feel that I am ready.  I'm not fazed by a visit to the Golf Club.  If hopes, dreams, fantasies, and all that I long for, collapse around me then I can shoulder the blame for my downfall.  In the end, I shall remain, some version of who I am now, Rosa Saint John.

**A small step forward**

I don't know what drives me to do such a thing but I go to visit my parents.  It's been a while.  I don't suppose they're going to throw a homecoming party and they may now believe disownment means disownment.

I knock on the door, enter in tiny steps.  I see them in familiar seats.  The interior looks clean so their new sweeping-brush-up-the-ass woman is doing a good job.

'It's Our Rosa,' says father – hell, he recognizes me!

'What do you want?' said mother coldly.

'How are you both?' I say.

'What do you care?' asks mother.

Father turns his head, 'She has been supporting Katy,' says father in my defense.

There's a silence.  Mother's twitching of her fingers tells me she's thinking.

'Katy is fine,' I say.

'Well...' begins mother.  'You'll know all the gossip... why has Brian gone?  There's more to it than she's telling us.'

'Relationships go stale,' I say.

'Ha!' scoffs mother.  'You'll know about that, won't you?'

'Mother,' yelps father scolding her.  He faces me, smiles, kind of nods to indicate he's forgotten the past.  If I want to be a whore, that's my business, and I'm still his daughter.

'Where has Brian gone?  You haven't been interfering... it's nothing to do with you...?'

'All I know is that they've parted.  Katy is getting on with her life.  She's okay,' I say.

'And are you okay, love?' says father.

Mother asks how Marty is going on and she's heard that he's changed his job.

There follows a few more questions, a few more brief answers and to a small degree, the frost that has existed for many months thaws a little.  Before I leave, I kiss father on top of his head.  My mother reminds me that there is more to life than 'cavorting' and I should get my priorities in order.  As I closed the door, they both shout, 'Bye, love' and the phrase 'time is a healer' springs to mind.


**A speech to Marty**

'I want you to listen... It's not often that I open up to you but I feel now is the time to clarify where we stand.  We've been through a lot... things are different from how they used to be.  It's no longer a case of you and me against the world... we're part of the world, and life goes on all around us.  Perhaps we've built bridges between us.  There isn't simplicity anymore – once others enter a relationship it becomes complicated; you think of more than me and I think of more than you.  That's how it goes, Marty, and we can't pretend otherwise.'

'Sure, you were maybe trying to repair this past year by asking me to marry you.  You tried; I admire you for that.  Maybe it was a rash act, you didn't think too much, you just saw a proposal as a sticking plaster – a solution to our problems.'

'But our problems, if you like to call them problems, run deeper.  We've both changed, both had experiences that the other knows nothing about.  And before you start thinking you'll tell me your secrets, and I'll tell you mine, and that will be some kind of remedy... don't even go there.  We'll believe what we want to believe, we'll start accusing each other of leaving out details.  We'll drift further apart... perhaps even part for good.'

'I want to tell you how I see us now, Marty.  You can accuse me of being wrong, but remember, I can accuse you of being a liar, and that will get us nowhere.  I see us now having a weird sort of friendship.  It's good of you to support me, it's good of you to let me live here, and yes, we have sex, we eat together sometimes, we sleep together, and maybe to the neighbors, we appear to be an ordinary couple.  Marty, ordinary couples don't share their bed.  Ordinary couples aren't made up of two people with conflicting ideas about what's going to make them happy. There's no doubt in my mind that presently you are more attracted to my sister than you are to me.  And that doesn't bother me, no Marty, if you think I'll be jealous or have a desire to go tear Katy's hair from her head, then you're wrong.  I don't mind at all if you're screwing Katy morning, afternoon and night. If you're both trying to deceive me, it's failing.  If you're trying to protect my feelings, then don't.  I've got issues of my own that are nothing to do with either you or Katy.  There're are things going on in my head that I wouldn't confess to a priest.'

'Marty, just as you and Katy need to learn where you stand with each other, I need to learn what I need to do to be satisfied.  I have ideas that materialized after your affair with Caroline.  And I'm not blaming you for me having them.  They came about from circumstance, they came about because not only you ventured further than the matrimonial bed, so did I.  And the journey I went on took me to places I never knew existed. What happened to me opened my eyes to what even a girl like me can experience in life.  It's not gone from my system.  At this moment in time, I couldn't so much as say with honesty if I like girls more than guys.  I couldn't tell you if I prefer one lover, two lovers, or ten lovers.  I couldn't tell you if I preferred you or anyone else on top of me or me on top of them.  It's complicated, Marty.  It's complicated, but I'm being honest with you, and you must understand that if you go doing what you wish to do – screwing Katy for instance – then you've got to expect me to be more than a domestic who shares your bed.  I intend to find myself, and whatever that means, I'm going to go forward – sometimes I may not be here, sometimes I may stay out for a night.  Are you listening, Marty?'

**A long drive to the twentieth hole**

I guess that Marty and Katy discussed my speech.  I guess it's immoral for me to use money given to me by Marty to use for taxis as I pursue my dreams – dreams!  Ha, I can hardly call what I search for a dream, but I've got to describe it somehow.  It's crazy how folks cling on to notions they see as future achievements when it's so easy to adopt another idea as to where to go, what to do.  If, last year, I'd not phoned Tracey minutes before she set off to the Golf Club and she asked me if I'd like to go along… if, if, if…. I'd not be doing this.  More likely at this time in the evening I'd be reading a magazine on the sofa, watching television, listening to Marty's tales from the office and being unaware that gang-bangs exist outside the porn industry.  In time, our perceptions of life alter – a sweet uncomplicated partner perceives the outside world differently to the whore I am now.

I wait for the cab outside the local shop.  I'm dressed 70% tart, 30% decent.  I'm already rehearsing lines I'll say to the first member that greets me, 'Hi, any chance of a second gang-bang – clear the tables and chairs, just leave one table in the middle, I'm ready when you are.'  I can't say I'll feel embarrassed or ashamed; they're a bunch of strangers now Brian's gone.  To be honest, I'm more concerned about coming away disappointed and receiving a thunderous 'No – fuck off, you tramp.'  The cab arrives; I tell the driver the name of the Golf Club eight miles away.

The information Tracey gave me last year was less than sketchy.  She mentioned no contact name, nor from whom she'd received the invitation.  We turned up after getting tipsy at a nearby pub, put on the show, and left with a members' donation of over four hundred quid.  If anyone asks me which of the members I know, I'll say, 'Line them up with their dicks hanging, I may pick one or two that I recognize.'

Jokes aside, as the cab gets closer, my fear of rejection rises.  I've spent too long persuading myself that this is the only way to satisfy my needs, I'd hate for it all to go wrong.  I spur myself on, 'You can do it, girl, you can do it.'  Tracey Cummings will be proud of me!

The cab pulls up.  I pay the fare.  I check my clothes, decide I'm 80% tart and 20% decent.  I hoist up my skirt and extra half-inch then go to the doorway where I and Tracey went before and as I open the heavy door some kind of odd thrill runs through my body.

I sigh with relief when I see that the same guy who met us last year is standing like a sentry in the foyer.  He smiles at me as if he thinks I'm lost.  'Can I help?' he says politely.'

'Do you know Tracey Cummings?' I say.

He looks me up and down, takes a pace backward, 'Are you the girl…?

'Yes,' I say.  'On the table… last July, or somewhere around July.'

He raises a finger, smiles again, 'One moment…'  Then he disappears through a nearby doorway and I'm left wondering if I'm completely prepared for an imminent act of depravity.  Now is as good a time as ever.  If I hear a round of applause, I'll know my luck is in.

After three minutes a smart man of around sixty walks toward me, places his hand on my back and asks if I'd care to accompany him to the pub fifty yards away.  He hurries me along as if he's not keen on being noticed by other members.  When we get outside, he introduces himself, 'I'm David, and you…'

'Rosa,' I say.

Inside the pub, he asks what I'd like to drink.  I ask for a gin.  He goes to the bar and in another minute, we're sitting at a small table and he's eyeing my body like it's a car he's thinking of buying.

'I take it that you are offering your services,' he says.  I nod.  'Unfortunately, last year, certain over-respectable members complained.  The fun parties at the Golf Club have ceased.  That is not to say I'm not interested in you.'

'Do you know, Tracey?' I ask.

He ignores the question.  'Have you ever worked, been employed?' he says.

'I worked in a café.'

'And how much did you earn?'

'Sometimes, one hundred and sixty pounds a week,' I say.

His eyebrows lift and stay high on his head.  'Would you like to earn that amount ten times over – in say three days?' he asks.

At first. I feel insulted that he's mentioned money.  I'm not a prostitute.  I didn't come here for the money.  Not too enthusiastically, I say, 'How?'

'I can arrange an introduction for you.  It depends on what you're prepared to do.'

'Anything,' I say.

'You don't have limits?'

'I wouldn't have called if I had limits.  Did you watch me and Tracey?'

'I did,' he says.  'Remarkable.  Girls like you are in demand.'

I don't know what else to say.  He takes a fifty-pound note from his wallet and slides it across the table.  He tells me it's for expenses.  Next, he takes a business card from another pocket. He slips it between my fingers.  'Call at the listed address the day after tomorrow – around ten in the morning.  Ask for Sonny.  Give him your name, he'll be expecting you.'

As soon as I look him in the eye, he gets up and leaves.  I think two things: what could a girl do with so much money and why did he ignore my question about Tracey?


**Without interruption**

I call at Katy's; she's working but halts when I go in.  She doesn't speak much; she's probably thinking that I'm going to raise the topic of her and Marty.  To settle her I plant a passionate kiss on her lips and tell her that I love her.  She makes a coffee and then I surprise myself by opening up about what I felt like being gang-banged by two or three dozen members of a Golf Club.

'It was like being in a conscious dream,' I say, 'one of those dreams that you hope will never end.  When I look back, I see flashes of faces, arms reaching out, hands smothering me, incredible noises that all merge into one chaotic sound.  There are bodies of men and women, naked flesh, erect dicks, and women without their knickers.  Each image lasts a second or two; they're ever-changing and rich with color.  But what I remember clearly is how I felt and how my body rose to another level of experience.  Thrills, magical sensations overran me, from the toes to the top of my head; my belly hungered, my thighs tingled and spasmed, my ass burned with excitement.  To know you're helpless is a glorious feeling.  And the more those folks did to me the more I wanted them to do.  I didn't want it to end, Katy.  And Katy… you know what, I want to be gang-banged again.  I need to know that it wasn't a dream and I need to recapture that feeling of being wholly fulfilled.'

She stroked my hair, neither encouraged me nor discouraged me.  She said she is my sister, no matter what.  She never mentioned Marty.  I told her I was looking for sex that is way beyond anything we've done together.  I asked her if she'd be there at the end to pick up the pieces.  She said that she would.


## A token of affection

The evening before my appointment I strapped Marty's wrists behind his back with his pink fluffy straps.  He didn't need a little blue pill.  He lay in the chair wearing a look of amazement.  I took an age to please him, and when he finally could hold on no longer, he released his pleasure and then moaned blissfully.  'What brought that on?' he said.

'I don't want you thinking I'm wasting my life.  I've renounced some of my skills, but I've acquired others.'


**In the balance**

It's a huge risk, I know, but dressing to kill will either succeed or fail dismally.  I take a huge gamble and wear my see-throughs with high heels and know I'm perhaps the first girl to dare traveling in daylight in such an outfit.  My tiny jacket conceals a small part of me but there's a good deal more on show.

The taxi driver has his eyes more on the rearview mirror than on the road.  Car drivers honk their horns as they pass.  I feel a little excited and look sensational and I'm making it clear that I want the job.  I'm dropped on one of the city's main thoroughfares and glared at in an instant.  An old man freezes and gawps at my crotch; younger men and women don't know where to fix their eyes.  I hear a boy cry, 'Hot stuff,' as he's pulled along by his mother and father.

I enter the 15 story block and glance at the business card: 14th floor, Sonny Mabon Associates.  At least I'm the only passenger in the elevator and have time to adjust my skirt and top.  I examine my reflection in the large mirror, smile approvingly then face the doors awaiting exit.  The doors open.  There is a large area with entrances to several businesses.  SMA is to my left and looks just like any other professional premises in the city.  There is no welcoming sign for tarts.

I press a buzzer, hear a click, then enter.  A middle-aged woman is the first to notice me; she's unflustered by my outfit.

'Rosa,' I say.  She smiles, leads me along a wide corridor until it widens into a large area where a very tanned man is relaxing at a very large desk.  He stands, gives me a quick inspection, then offers me a seat.

'I'm a friend of Tracey Cummings?' I say.

He looks vacant, then glances at my tits as if I've suddenly awakened his interest.

'So… it's Rosa.'

'Rosa Saint John.'

'Age?'

'26.'

'You are in good condition for 26,' he says.  'No children.'

'No children.'

'And you are prepared to work…?'  I give him a glum stare – what's that supposed to mean?  'You'd like me to take a look at you?'

'Weren't you at the Golf Club last year?' I ask.

'Unfortunately, not,' he says.  Then he ponders, his eyes pierce my soul as he swivels a pencil between his fingers.  He leans forward, opens my jacket to see more of me, and says, 'Is there anything that you are not willing to do.  I must know now. Speak while you can.'

'No,' I say without thinking.  'I'll do anything.'

'Good,' he says, then he stands and leads me to a subsection of the large area.

There is a large white backscreen behind a platform.  The middle-aged woman introduces herself as Angela, then a guy with a camera and a woman dressed as a nurse enter from another room.  Sonny retreats and I suddenly feel like a guinea pig in the company of three mad scientists.

Angela taps her hand on a tabletop. 'Clothes,' she says sharply.

I wonder what she means until I see the guy playing with his camera and realize I'm next in line for a photo-shoot – a naked photoshoot at that! God, what's going on? Little wonder the pay is more than the minimum wage.

I strip off, place everything on the table including my heels. As soon as I'm naked the nurse-like creature grabs my arms and leads me to a fucking hospital bed in the far corner of the room. She lays me on my front and doesn't waste a second before feeling my flesh, every part of me, and quite roughly. Then she turns me over, yanks open my legs and inspects my pussy. From pussy to belly, from belly to tits, from tits to neck and ears. Hell, do they desire to breed from me? 'Do I pass?' I say sarcastically. The nurse-like creature nods at Angela; Angela points to the platform – get on there, honey, and show us your credentials.

The photographer tells me to stand facing him, put my weight on one leg, on the other legs, extend my tits, hold my hips, with a wide stance, cover my tits, stroke my pussy, turn and show my ass, bend, expose, look sexy, do you want clients to screw you or not – part your fucking cheeks!

I think I've earned a grand already.

Fifteen minutes then Angela dismisses the menials. She reads from a list attached to a clipboard the longest lists of sexual variations I've ever heard. Some, I've never heard of. 'Do you object to any of these,' she says. 'I must know now. Speak while you can,' she says. Haven't I heard this line previously?

I dress, get returned to Sonny who mutters about me being 26. Most girls are younger than me. He has clients who go for older women. Thanks, sweet-talker. He tells me he'll get feedback on the photos.  If I'm accepted, he'll give me three four-hour sessions a week.  The more I get chosen, the more I'll earn.  Simple as that.  I'll be picked up and taken to another location.  He gets me to fill in a form to record my required pick-up point and other details.  I choose a local shop.  Just before he lets me go, he scans my body, licks his lips and says, 'Love the outfit, babe… wear it for work occasionally.'

And that's it.  No explanations as to what I'll do – it's obviously not milking cows – or where I'll be working from.  He didn't mention the money.  He didn't say if I'd be screwing old millionaires or offered to a football crowd for two 45 minute halves.  The thought that they seemed satisfied with my body pleased me.  I'm left a little puzzled.  Maybe I should have asked more questions.

I intended to go home, but half-way home I told the cabbie to drive to Katy's house.  Frustration was building and I felt in need of attention.  I burst into Katy's and yelled that if she didn't help me, I'd destroy Marty's supply of little blue pills.  She was horrified to learn I'd been to town in my see-throughs.  I threatened that I'd run naked up and down her street unless she soothed me.  Her horror faded.  And the result is that I got one victory today.


**Messages to the unresponsive**

One simple question has been haunting me; why didn't David or Sonny Mabon respond when I asked them about Tracey Cummings?  If I went into the street and asked two strangers if they knew Sally, the girl with the purest most gorgeous body in the neighborhood, they'd say 'yes' or 'no'. If I asked if they knew Father Christmas, I get an answer.

I text Tracey, 'I've been to the Golf Club – want to know what happened?'

Ten minutes later, another text, 'I talked with David. I asked about you.'

An hour passes. I know she looks at her texts. Why the silence?

Another text. 'David sent me to see a guy in town – Sonny Mabon. I dropped your name. Isn't Tracey Cummings famous?'

I wait some more. I curse her for not replying. Then I send my longest text, 'It's SO OBVIOUS THAT YOU STILL LOVE ME. Why are you ignoring me? If you haven't stopped loving me by now, you never will. Text me you bitch. Let's get it on soon.'

I simply don't understand why she doesn't reply, unless as I've said that she's still battling with the pain of love. She daren't face me or call me. She knows that she'll crumble.


**Wading through hours of uncertainty**

There can be nothing worse than a death row prisoner awaiting a last-minute stay of execution. Stop the execution of the judgment, he cries, but no-one hears him in his isolation. Oh, I'm not comparing my predicament to his, but the hours go by and I get tired of thinking. What if this? What if that? What if I spend the next fifty years failing to discover who I am or who I want to be? Not hearing from Sonny is making me nervous. I try to put my job interview to the back of my mind, shelved on the same shelf as Tracey Cummings, but I fail. When I sit and ponder, I feel like folks from my present, past and future are whizzing by me, slowing down, falling behind, then accelerating again.  No-one remains at my side.  Do I want them to?  Do I need them to?  Am I a girl running away from stability because I once tried it and it failed me?  When there was me and Marty, problems like this didn't exist.  I had ordinariness, routine; I lacked dreams and ambition.  My fortune then was a cozy evening in bed with my partner and a glass of wine, watching television, him jokingly asking me for something other than salad for his meal after work.

I gaze from my room window and see pedestrians pass whose lives are simple.  I see mothers with their kids exchanging loving smiles, men whistling, smoking cigarettes and enjoying the cough that clears their lungs.  Taxis sometimes halt at the opposite side of the street and the drivers nod their head to music on car radios.  There are constant reminders that my life is unlike other lives – I'm waiting to qualify as a paid whore and I don't know if my grades are good enough.

Then I question whether this job is going to be all I desire.  Money has never motivated me.  If it turns out that I'm scheduled to have one on one sex with old rich men once, twice, three times each evening, then I'm hardly going to rejoice and sing the praises of Sonny Mabon Associates from the rooftops.  Pay with pleasure is bollocks!  Pleasure without pay is more appealing.  I ask myself why I didn't construct a rota: 10 am – go to the brothers for a double up, noon – dine on Sally's body until early afternoon, 3 pm – entertain myself on the kitchen table, 6 pm – (childcare provided) threesome with Marty and Katy, and 9 pm – all locals invited for a nightly orgy in a bedroom of choice.  Days off at Christmas only.

Why the fuck am I waiting for someone to decide my future.  The frustration grows and I resort to desperate measures.

One morning I go to the top end of Katy's street via the park and hang about for an hour hoping to see Sally.  No Sally.  With the taste of her on my tongue, I walk quickly to her door, hammer on the woodwork and half-believe I'm going to pounce on her body the second she opens the door.  I'll give her no choice – sex all day and I'll promise to leave before Harry gets home.  Sally doesn't come to the door; Sally is out or hiding.

But worse was to come.  I craved for punishment.  I had a longing to be hurt mentally because I began to think that Sonny Mabon had rejected me on the grounds of age – 26 is too old to gain favor from men who like their women barely women who've just stepped up from puberty.  So, when Marty said he wasn't working one afternoon I ordered him to call Katy to call at our house.  When she got here, I looked the pair of them squarely in the eye and said I wanted to watch them have sex on our sofa.  I gave them the reason that I loved them; watching them would make me happy and I deserved something special because I hadn't interfered with how they were carrying on.  Sure, they were mystified and felt uncomfortable getting undressed as I sat like a film director in the armchair.  I told them how to screw.  I told them when to change position, and I watched, sometimes in mild pain, as my partner did all I asked of him to my sister.  God, that's kind of sick and I'm a little surprised that one of them didn't rebel.  I suppose the more I felt certain that the job wasn't going to happen, and if it did happen it would be a let-down, the more perverted ideas ran through my head.  I even wondered what it would be like to somehow lure Sally to our bedroom, and me, Marty and Katy all having a huge piece of her.  Oh, a girl like Sally isn't for sharing, but when the mind is in overdrive it invents all sorts of scenarios.

Three days after my interview – yes, three whole days! – I received a text: BE AT YOUR REQUESTED PICK-UP POINT 9.15. FAILURE TO COMPLY WILL RESULT IN DISMISSAL.


**9.10pm to 10.10pm**

Nightclubbing – believe it or not, Marty, Rosa Saint John is springing to action.

I'm dressed in my see-throughs with a different pair of heels.  I'm wearing scarlet lipstick, face powder that makes me look whiter than white, and feel like a five-star tart who's heading off on a one-star adventure.  If I'm too disappointed I'm determined to quit – they can't dismiss me for being over-qualified.

At 9.12 two teenage lads see me and ask if I charge for a shag.  They're still inside the local shop when a Volvo pulls up three minutes later; a window opens, and a young guy in smart clothes calls my name.  I sit on the rear seat.  I get the impression he's not supposed to talk.  After three questions I give up searching for conversation.  He obeys company rules – he's much to learn in life.

He drives on roads I've never traveled on.  Almost twenty minutes pass before he turns onto a narrow lane and drives by a gatehouse; we're entering some kind of grounds where a mansion-type building sits about 400 yards from the main road.  It's not what I expected; the building reminds me of something from a horror film.  Several cars are scattered around a spacious area to the right side of the house.

I'm told to enter through an archway; I'll be met by a maid.  Jesus – a maid!

And inside the house a plain young woman with a black dress and white pinafore and white hat greets me.  'Follow me, Rosa,' she says like someone at a funeral parlor.  This is creepy; I'm expecting to see a butler carrying a silver tray holding wine glasses.  The interior is dimly lit and I can hear my heels clopping on the floorboards.

The maid leads me up two flights of a wide staircase.  The building appears larger from the inside; there are corridors, open spaces, many doorways; it's like a museum without the exhibits, a library without books.  Again, I attempt small-talk but the maid is stony silent.

She opens a large door and she briefly shows me the girls' preparation room.  There are girls in various stages of undress, and what strikes me is not only their beauty, but hell, I don't see one who looks much older than twenty.  One girl is parading like she's a princess and telling the other girls to watch her tits.  'See, they don't move,' she brags, then the maid hurries me along.  We pass two more maids before arriving at a wide corridor that's in darkness.  The maid flicks a switch on the wall and on comes six spotlights, the narrow beams shoot individually from the left side of the corridor to illuminate six black metal-barred cages on the right-side wall.  There is a red carpet down the center.  I get goosebumps, get feelings of trepidation when the maid uses a large key to open the huge lock of the first cage.  She points to a set of manacles hanging from a hook at the deepest point of the cage.  Then takes from a tiny shelf a black blindfold.  She demonstrates how to place the blindfold on the head and secure the wrists in the manacles.  There is a specific way I should stand before clients come to view: hands aloft in the manacles, palms touching, arms straight, head tilted, legs posed with one knee in front of the other.  I must not smile, nor fidget.  The hook on the wall can be pushed up and down to allow for a girl's height.  There is a buzzer close to the foot chance I need to pee.  A maid will come for me.  A buzzer will sound two minutes before clients appear on the corridor.  When a girl has been selected and the client has taken her to his required chamber, two buzzes will signal I may relax until I hear the next buzzer.  I must press the foot buzzer if I sweat, or for other purposes.  The buzzer must never be pressed when clients are present.  I shall get used to the routine.  She steps ahead of me, informs me that nine girls work six cages.  After a girl is selected her cage is filled by a reserve.  When I am on reserve duty, I must wait in the preparation room.

She takes me further along the corridor where there are many doors.  She says that all doors lead to various modes of entertainment for clients.  I must do exactly as a client or clients request.  When they have finished with me, the visitor/visitors leave through the entrance door.  I leave through a rear door that opens onto a corridor that in turn leads to the showering facility.  After each encounter, I must shower thoroughly before returning via another corridor to the preparation room.

We go along these corridors then I'm faced by the girls standing naked and in a line.  Another maid leads out six girls to fill six cages.  I am beginning my first four-hour shift as a reserve.  I must be ready.  Then I ask why the blindfolds are necessary.  'To protect clients' privacy,' she says obviously.  'Beyond this room and the rear areas, you must never remove a blindfold unless specifically asked to by a client.'

By 10.10 pm I'm sitting on a sofa stark naked with two young girls with bodies as wonderful as Sally's.  I keep glancing in their direction; the blonde girl is magnificent with cute little tits and the ginger-haired girl with freckles would look fabulous in straps on my bed.  Hey, I never asked if all clients are male.  Give me six of these girls and I'll be over the moon.


## Work: backache and money for old rope

I can't log the minutes; we're not allowed to hold phones, there is no clock, only the coming and going of maids who do not communicate.  Girls aren't particularly chatty; they seem keen on the money rather than sex.  The ginger girl is studying law at university and the blonde lives with her grandparents.  It's off-putting when the blonde tells me that on her first shift, she didn't earn a cent.  No clients picked her and she went home feeling ugly.  I tell her she's gorgeous.  'I'd screw you any day so long as you didn't charge me a fortune.'  She giggles sweetly before getting called to cage 3.  I'm told I'm the next reserve.  I sit hoping to hear 50 paratroopers running up the stairs.  Alas, the only sound is the girl who's been in cage 3 trotting into the preparatory room drying her body with towels.  She goes over to the mirrors where there's a unit that contains make-up, hairdryers, and the like and she boasts that she got a decent tip from an easy-to-handle client.  Is that a two-pound coin or a twenty-pound note?  No idea.  I'm learning slowly, but as yet I haven't had work.

The ginger girl tells me to be patient; it's worth the wait – she daren't tell me how much she's earned in the past three months and her grandfather thinks the university pays her for studying.

When I get summoned to cage 1 an elephant in my belly starts doing somersaults.  My finger ends tremble as I'm locked in the cage.  A different maid asks me if I know what to do.  'Be ready for when the buzzer sounds,' she says quite friendly with the voice of a child.

I rehearse the routine, blindfold, manacles, get the posing perfect, and when my body is elongated and revealing all its delights, I fantasize that I'd select myself for a screwing if I were a client.  Sure, those other girls are mouth-watering eye-candy but do they desire sex as much as I do?

I don't find it uncomfortable dangling from the hook. Knowing my body is highlighted by the spotlight is a turn on.  And maybe the biggest turn-on is the blindfold – the Devil himself may pick me and I am not going to know until his horns are penetrating my flesh.

The first voices I hear are those of a maid and a middle-aged man.  He selects a girl two or three cages away.  When the key turns in the lock it sends a shiver down my spine, and I urge myself to be patient, my turn will come!

I wait, tremble slightly, feel the coldish air brush my skin. The buzzer sounds and two minutes later, from afar, Japanese male voices are nearing.  The polite tones of a maid direct them. They shuffle along the line of cages, passing comments and making sounds of hunger.  When I feel they are standing outside my cage I try to present my body in its most favorable pose.  They hesitate, squabble mildly, before I hear a hand bang on the cage, 'This one, this one,' he says.  Oh God, I'm about to be screwed and I feel like yelling in gratitude.

The key unlocks the door.  A pair of strong hands fixes on my waist and lifts me like a butcher taking a carcass from a rail.  A different hand squeezes my ass as I'm led to the corridor.  I sense that a maid is steering the men to the room they have requested. Nothing can describe how I feel; I'm wanting them to be rough with me, hoping they'll think of me as a worthless whore.  They prod with their fingers, snatch at my hair though not violently. I hear the room door close. There's a rapid outburst of Japanese words, then suddenly my blindfold is pulled off and two men bow their heads.

"Konbanwa,' they say in turn.

I bow respectfully, before catching the sight of a harness suspended from the ceiling. One of the men touches the manacles as if he wants me to remove them. I oblige, then I spread my arms as if to say, 'Now do what you like with me.'

I'm stunned by their efficiency; they're regulars and know the procedure of getting a girl in a harness. It takes them two minutes to strap my ankles and wrists and have me suspended facing upward about five feet from the floor. They don't waste time; every part of my body becomes a plaything; they explore me, circle me, take it in turns to use their fingers between my legs. They cause me no harm, they are as considerate as Marty in the old days, and I'm at ease and being lulled into a false sense of security. A short while later, they lower the harness so I'm dangling about three feet from the ground. I get the idea they discuss who should go first; the tallest guy stiffens a hand and invites the other guy to screw me. The small guy wanders to my head and parts my mouth with his thumb and index finger. Then quite gently I'm being fucked from both ends. It's pleasant without being exciting and it goes on for perhaps five minutes before I get an inclination that things are about to change. There are more rapid words, gesticulations, and lots of repeated nods. They lower me to the floor, begin to untie my wrists and ankles and I notice their faces wear new expressions. Here comes the unexpected, I think, then they roll me onto my front and I realize what is happening.

What is happening is I'm getting hoisted from the floor while I'm facing downward.  I've not been raised six inches before the pain in the lower back and hips get me believing this is some kind of torture.  Again, they raise me about three feet; I sense they are more turned on; they are rougher, and it is now my ass that is the prime attraction, closely followed by my mouth.  Their dicks are harder and seem to have expanded by at least an inch. They don't warm-up, I'm pounded, drilled and annihilated from one end to the other.  After a minute they swap positions, keep on swapping, keep on battering me with their rigid bodies that don't appear to tire.  It's fabulously painful and erotically satisfying.  Somehow, I even manage to widen the distance between my thighs and get my head angled for the maximum entry.  They grunt loudly, and when I get the feeling that I'm taking everything they can force on me, I feel victorious.  I feel like asking for more, insulting their efforts as being second-rate.  I'm Rosa the whore.  I've been gang-banged, don't you know?

And when they are satisfied and believe I've taken their punishment, they lower me, untie the straps, and bow once more. The tall guy places two banknotes in my hand.  Another minute, then they are departing.  I collect the manacles and blindfold and leave by the rear door, along the narrow corridor and to the showering area.  I'm somewhat pleased.  One job is done – how many more before it's home time?

There are two different girls in the preparation room. They're wearing bathrobes and show me where to get one; it's moderately cold – we need to keep our bodies warm; 'There are no Eskimo clients,' jokes the slender girl.  They are friendly without being familiar.  One sounds posh, the other is a giggler who laughs continuously.  We are served refreshments by one of the maids who looks no more than fifteen-years-old.  I'm starting to feel comfortable.  I'm starting to think that this could be a career, at least until I reach 27.

I've no idea how long it is before I get locked in cage 4 and it doesn't take too long before I get selected again, but this time the client is less easy to identify.  Barely a word is spoken.  A maid says, 'Yes, sir,' but nothing else.  The cage is unlocked, I'm led very slowly along the corridor by what I think is a tall older man with wrinkled skin.  After a few paces, I think that the man must be very old or have a walking disability.  He keeps silent, doesn't touch my body or the manacles and blindfold.  The doorway we enter is closer than the previous one.  I stop and wait for him to remove the blindfold.  He doesn't.  I think about speaking but it is not allowed unless we are questioned.

Then I feel a hand on my back guiding me a few paces across the room.  I'm turned, pressure is applied to my shoulders and I'm encouraged to sit.  I imagine it to be some strange highchair with a V-shaped seat and a high flat back support.  As soon as my thighs are even on the rests, two rings curl around them and the top point of the V retracts leaving me like I'm sitting on some unusual toilet.  I can't sense where the man is and I've no idea what he's going to do to me.  There's a long pause and nothing happens until I hear the whirling of a motor.  Inside the next few seconds, I feel the top of a rubber dildo pressing onto my pussy.  I attempt to get my manacled hands between my thighs to direct the dildo where it's attempting to go.  It's awkward but I manage to succeed.  All the while I'm guessing where the man is standing but to be honest, I don't have a clue.  I can't hear him breathing and he's not moving about.

Then the machine starts to screw me, slowly at first, barely penetrating my body.  Sure, it's relaxing and the only distraction is trying to figure out what the guy is up to.  I'm expecting an onslaught, but what kind of onslaught, I don't know.

The machine gets faster with deeper insertions.  After five or ten minutes I'm getting incredibly horny and I can feel my lips parting and filling with blood.  Soon, I'm on the verge of an orgasm and not caring about the client but more for my own satisfaction.  My body begins writhing, my thighs are shaking like crazy, I'm as wet as a skinned fish but the machine doesn't know that I'm satisfied and keeps on and on screwing me.  It's insane; the guy hasn't touched me and I'm experiencing first-rate sex.  I increase my determination to cum again, soak up this new experience and if he suddenly does something outrageous well it could be a bonus.  And then...

I hear the door open and close.  I raise my manacled hands to the blindfold and take a peep.  He's gone, but for another two minutes, I make the most of the big rubber dildo.  Nobody told me to stop.  No-one said a client must watch me to the very end.  When I'm done, I find two more banknotes on the floor in front of the chair.  What a job, eighty quid up and it's quite a while until payday.

And then the routine begins again, shower, preparation room, wait.  But being screwed by a machine was my last assignment of the night.  At 1.30 am a maid called my name and said my driver was waiting downstairs.  I was free to go, 'See you the day after tomorrow,' she said.


**Post first working day**

I've journeyed to a different world.  From 9.10 to the moment I got home, I dwelt beyond a familiar existence in some sphere of make-belief.  I forgot about my real existence.  I felt that I moved in a circle beyond my understanding; to everyone at the isolated building a business operated, folks functioned as they do in societies that belong to works of fiction but not in the world of ordinary girls like Rosa Saint John.  When I worked in the café with Josivini, to receive a 50p tip would be unthinkable - receiving two tips totaling eighty pounds is astonishing.  I enjoy sex, I desire sex; to be tipped when the clients have already paid for the privilege of owning my body for a short time is ludicrous.  Had I been summoned to give my body for free, then I'd most likely have agreed.

As soon as I alighted from the Volvo outside the local store the realization that the boundaries of co-existing worlds can be crossed.  In some ways, I guess, it was akin to returning from an exotic holiday I'd won in a magazine competition – from fantasy to regularity in a single journey.

When I lay in bed next to Marty and picked out dark familiar shapes on the bedroom walls I thought of the spotlights and how I'd been highlighted like some special gift in a store window.  It's an extraordinary sensation hoping to be selected; when I was chosen I felt as though I'd won; I'd been favored over younger girls, more stunning girls, girls whose bodies are divine and whose faces still bear the look of innocence.  It's an ego boost, a thrill to carry to the grave.  I think above all things that happened, those two moments of selection are the prize features.


**A long walk to nowhere**


The most amazing aspect of the morning was the way I dressed.  I dug out an old pair of jeans, a masculine type shirt, and a pair of old trainers to disguise myself as an anonymous waif who could be on her way to the job center.  There's probably a psychological reason as to why, but I didn't stop to analyze.  I left the house around ten and set off on a long walk to nowhere.  Where is nowhere?  Nowhere is the place to go when there is no-one suitable to listen to confessions.  Nowhere is any place my feet are willing to tread.  I walk, stare at the pavement a few yards ahead, and when the pavement ends, I stare at the road, and when that ends I find my eyes are wandering along the path to the riverbank where last year I screwed Tracey and failed to screw Vini.  I stop when I reach the water.  The flowing river brings music to my ears.  The smell of the countryside is a refreshment and that sense of being isolated brings comfort.

I'm not there for more than two or three minutes before I take my clothes off and stand legs apart to gaze at my shivering reflection on the surface of the water.  I think about swimming to the other side.  I think about touching myself.  I recall how Tracey was scared of the water because she couldn't swim well.  I think about Katy and what she'd make of me here, alone and naked.

I bet all folks at some time have done crazy things. Secrets are tiny treasures never to be revealed.  If you make a secret darker it is harder to share, so I lay on the riverbank and enriched my secret with self-fulfillment – who gives a shit; it's just another confession that's not going to be told.  Then I laugh at the girl I used to be – Rosa Naivety Saint John, simple, a devoted daughter, docile partner, her who fit into the crowd and couldn't be seen.

From the riverbank, a three-mile walk to the council estate and a trek along the street where Tracey Cummings lives – sometimes, perhaps, only sometimes?  Then across the field, along the lane behind the church, up to my parents' house where

I consider calling but decline because there is a car parked outside
– whose car, I don't know.  My legs then carry me to Katy's where
she's plonking swiftly on her keyboard.  She's warm but I realize
that I'm interrupting her flow.  We exchange words that have little
meaning.  'The girls are at school?' I say.  They are so obviously at
school.  She notices how I'm dressed and assumes I'm not happy.
I make up jokes to prove that I am.  She offers me a coffee – I
decline on the grounds of needing to go home and finish the
laundry.

What a contrast!  Killing time in the freedom of everyday
life.  What a contrast to being the meat in a sandwich for two
Japanese gentlemen and the source of thrills for an old guy who
quits before I do.

Is it better taking long walks to nowhere or short walks
blindfolded in manacles?  Right now, grant me the wish to pass all
my days posed in a metal cage ready to be chosen, and I'll take it.
The clients can screw me upside down, ten at a time, bound,
gagged and chained, for an hour or until I lose consciousness.  I
don't care, but it's a more stimulating prospect than watching the
washing machine on full-spin with a sweeping brush up my ass
ready to clean the floors.


## A generous offer

Marty asks me what I think about having another threesome with
Katy.  I respond by querying if Katy wants me in the threesome.
'Maybe she prefers you and her?  Maybe she knows that it's
because of her your little blue pills are redundant?'

He doesn't know how to reply.  Katy doesn't have a babysitter for tonight.  Does he think her daughters will sit on the sofa while their mum is sprawled frog-like screaming on our bed?

'What about tonight?' says Marty.

'I'm going out,' I say.

'Until early morning again?' he says.

'Sure, I told you I was searching for myself – I haven't yet found me and I'm determined to keep on looking.'

'I thought you loved being with your sister?'

'Not as much as you do, buster.  Invite her, screw her ass, but don't moan if her girls keep on interrupting.'

He sits in his armchair and starts tapping his fingers on his knee.


**Back on the job**

The ginger-haired girl, the blonde, and I were the first three in line to occupy the cages.  I didn't have to wait long before a pair of middle-aged lesbians decided I was to be their treat for the evening.  I was asked to remove the manacles, informed that it was Thelma's 50th birthday and as you don't get to fifty every day, the pair had vowed to celebrate by sharing a nice young woman with a lovely smooth pussy and a firm ass.  The ass was important; my ass fitted their image of what a nice ass should look like.

But when the women removed their clothes as I laid on an extra-large bed, I suddenly realized that sex with older women wouldn't be like sex with Sally.  I think the non-Thelma saw my expression; kindly, she asked if I'd like to wear the blindfold; she could hide her embarrassment by me not seeing what she does to me.  I smiled, covered my eyes, and as the old saying goes, laid back and thought of England.

Most of their concentration was on my lower half.  To be frank, I dreaded being sat upon and hated the feel of their saggy flesh.  Sure, they were pleasant enough women and they got me wondering what I'll be like at their age.  If I take to procuring young girls for sex then I'll allow them to wear blindfolds to ward off their feelings of revulsion.  I received a twenty-pound tip in exchange for a final squeeze of my ass.  They departed both satisfied and claimed they were going home to drink a full bottle of vintage port.

I went along the back corridor, showered, then returned to the preparatory (yes, preparatory, I'm told – not preparation) room where two girls I'd not spoken to before were playfully stroking each other's thighs.  They waved, said, 'Hi' then joined me at the mirrors.  They had bathrobes hanging on their shoulders but in a mirror, I couldn't stop ogling their gorgeous bodies; most of the girls were fabulously shaped and all with very pretty faces.  'Super belly,' said the nearest girl complimenting me.

I folded back her robe, 'Super everything,' I said.  Then I did the same to the other girl and I think I left some kind of impression – likely my eyes told them I wouldn't mind selecting the pair of them from a cage, with or without manacles and blindfolds.

But then came a chilling moment that knocked me sideways.  The girls moved away and I opened one of the drawers of the unit under the mirrors looking for make-up.  The very first thing I see is a tiny pale blue pouch that is split on one corner of the seam.  It's like viewing a ghost.  I'm sure I gulped and drew in a breath.  An identical pouch used to sit on the top of the drawers

in Tracey Cummings bedroom; it held a single green lipstick that
we once used to write filthy words on each other's naked bodies
before having insane sex first thing one Wednesday morning.  My
insides trembled.  How many pouches like this one exist in Leeds?
Immediately, I ask the girls if they know of a Tracey.

'Yes, there's a Tracey,' says one.

'Big tits Tracey,' says the other.

'What does she look like?' I ask without hearing the
adjective.

'Big tits,' repeats the second girl.

'Tallish, dark hair,' says the first.

That's not a description that fits Tracey but I'm not
reassured that a ghost hasn't visited this room in the past.  I
become quiet, and for a while, stop thinking about getting back in
a cage; I'm half-believing that Tracey may have followed my path,
first to the Golf Club and then to Sonny Mabon Associates.  I put
the pouch in the pocket of my jacket at my changing area, then sit
solemnly waiting for my turn to be called.

As with my first day, I get chosen twice.  The second time
is by three youngish city bankers (at least that's what they looked
like) who took me to a room with an assortment of frames and
what's best described as wooden lean-overs.  They were only
interested in my ass, 'Bend over there, spread your legs,' – of
course they didn't say that; they just ragged me about like an
object and competed to see which one could make me scream
loudest.  They constantly bickered for the one hammering me to
stop, 'It's my turn, it's his turn, I want her ass, we'll keep screwing
her until her body bursts.'  I ended up with my head and wrists
trapped in stocks while they worked off their energy.  It proved
pretty brutal.

I'd have enjoyed the sex more if I hadn't found the pouch, though it did surprise me that when they'd finished with me, they rolled up five twenty pound notes and stuck them up my ass. 'You're a doll,' one said as they left. I had to be released by a maid who came to find me. By the time I'd showered and returned to the preparatory room another maid was telling me that my driver waited downstairs. One hundred and twenty pounds in tips is mightily pleasing.

## Emotional needs

It's funny how emotions fluctuate, one minute a girl can be up in the air, the next she's down in the dumps licking her wounds, and she's unsure where those wounds are in her body. I've been through so many highs and lows that my heart doesn't know how to beat with regularity. I require love and compassion. I'm no longer sure where I belong and I feel as lost as I did in early spring when wandering the streets of Torquay before I went to Brighton.

Is it Marty's house or our house? Madly I think that I was happy in Sally's caravan. Ridiculously, I even admit that when I slaved to keep my parents' house clean, I felt a touch of contentment. Do I belong in a cage or behind the counter in a café? Do I want to feel loved or sexually satisfied? Up, down, like the waves on an ocean. I'm a raging sea and calm, calm waters. I'm the river that's endlessly emptying its waters without knowing what kind of waters are coming to replenish me.

God, what's gone wrong? Finding what is maybe Tracey's green lipstick pouch has unsettled me. I'd always believed that I hankered after Tracey because she is the only person, apart from Katy, who truly loves me. It was never a case of me being madly in love with her, more an appreciation of her love for me.  The pouch seems to have shattered those ideas.  I inspect the pouch as if it's Tracey's body.  I sniff it, stroke it, and I've spoken to it.  Crazy.  I'm shredded and in need of love from someone.

And I'm forced to admit too that after only two shifts at Sonny Mabon Associates my desperate craving to be gang-banged has wilted to a moderate desire.  There are a few reasons I can think of: (A) I don't have any hope of it happening – I doubt that a vast crowd of clients is going to turn up together and pick me in cage number whatever (B) I'm receiving a steady stream of mild sexual satisfaction (C) earning money (D) my compass is spinning and I don't presently know in which direction it's going to settle.

I need a counselor, a psychotherapist, a brain mechanic, and a witch doctor to offer me advice.  Rescue me… take me in your arms and rescue me.

Katy says she can spare an hour for a chat and two cups of coffee.  I go there in giant strides, again dressed in old jeans and an old shirt.  Instinctively she knows her sister is Rosa the Confused – 'Why the dull expression?  Why the arched shoulders?  You've been in my house a full minute and you're yet to mention sex," says Katy.

I fall into her arms and start sobbing like a double-busted waste pipe.  'Has Marty said something?  Have you been to our parents'?  What happened last night when you were at the night clubs?'

'I wasn't at the night clubs…' I say.

'You weren't up to your old tricks?' she asks squeezing me on her breasts.

'It's nothing related to anything but me,' I plead.

'I love you, Rosa.'

Oh, it's hard to relay how much her words meant to me. I lifted my wet face and kissed her on the lips. 'I love you, Katy. It seems like there's only us two who know what love is.'

She guides me to the sofa, forgets the coffee, moves strands of wet hair from my cheeks. 'Do you want me to take you to bed?' she says.

I laugh as I'm crying. 'That's the first time you've said that.'

'I hate to see you unhappy.'

I kiss her again then try to focus. 'I'm not unhappy now, big sis. If you keep on holding me, I'll be okay.'

And on the sofa, we cuddled until my heart was warmed with love. I never mentioned my work, Tracey Cummings, or what was going on between her and Marty. We must have kissed twenty times and each time our lips met I felt love transfuse from her body to mine. We didn't speak a whole lot; our breasts were heating but we didn't head for the bedroom. When Katy allowed me to kiss her neck it seemed that my woes had been forgotten. I'd like to record that a passionate love scene followed, but we drank a coffee, then I let her get on with her accounting.


**Unpredictable, that's what you are**

Didn't I say that life is full of ups and downs... the unimaginable happened. Yes, I mean the unimaginable happened and got my juices flowing like they haven't flowed in a long, long time.

I'd cooked Marty a meal, delivered it to his lap on a tray then relaxed on our sofa with a glass of orange juice. I am thinking about work, sort of musing about what may be contained in the rooms that no clients have taken me. I half-fantasize about contraptions, wonder what's the weirdest thing a client can do to a girl's body and what could be done to mine that would send me to heaven.

Marty asks what I'm thinking about. I'm blunt, 'Filthy sex,' I say.

He tells me to come up with some ideas. That's typical, always my ideas – why didn't I shack up with someone with a vivid imagination?

Then... I'm two seconds from having my thighs shook.

I receive a text message.

It's got to be...

'Hi, how are you. Sally X'

I adjust my sitting position and Marty looks up. This is the first text I've ever, ever received from Sally. My mind throws up images of me feasting on her body – a body as beautiful as those young girls in the cages at SMA. My fingertips hover over the screen; they're twitching.

'Who's that?' asks Marty.

'Only one of the girls from the Fat Club,' I say.

'I thought you quit the Fat Club.'

'I did.'

'I'm fine. How is my favorite landlady?' I text back.

'I was wondering...' she replies.

Hey, don't hold back, girl. Sally is missing me. 'Do you want SEX?'

'Please,' is her response.

'I hunger for you,' I text.

'Good.'

'If we meet, can I go at you without restrictions?'

'What's that mean?'

'Fuck you until your legs won't support you.'

'I'd like that,' she texts.

I ask if she'd like to come to my house on Monday morning. There'll be no-one here from 8 am to 5 pm. We'll have lots of time. She can shower if she needs to. I send her my address and put in capitals I WANT YOUR BODY.'

'Thanks, Rosa. I'll be there after nine.'

'Can't wait. X.'

'You have a lot to say to her,' says Marty.

'She wants ideas for exercise,' I tell him.


**Two good ends to the week**

With blues dispelled and spirits healed I go to my last shift of the week in a mood to be pleased. I'll take whatever comes my way and enjoy it. I harbor the idea that there's a vague similarity between having sex with the person who knows how best to thrill me (Tracey Cummings) and the one whom I most enjoy thrilling (Sally). The former is a master at dishing out punishment and the latter, if I have my way, will become the recipient of mine. Go for it, girl – let the fun begin.

Although I'm the first reserve there's no long wait to be screwed by a guy in his thirties who likes me in manacles but insists on seeing all my face. I get impaled on a bed, pulled to the edge, pulled more when he raises my legs and then rewarded with thirty pounds as he asks for my name and phone number. I'm not allowed to give him my number. 'Choose me next time,' I say as he leaves.

It's a busy night, lots of buzzers, girls in the preparatory room counting their cash and reapplying make-up. I see the girl who must be Big Tits Tracey – I wouldn't care for that weight on my chest but some guys love melons and medicine balls.  She gets clients and that's all that matters.

When I'm next in the cage I pray for a trio of my-age lesbians; unfortunately, from gossip I've heard female clients tend to be older.  I get another single guy around forty with a square jaw and big muscles who's led me to the room I first visited with the Japanese guys.  He knows what to do and barely acknowledges that I'm with him until he surprises me from behind by picking me up and turning me upside down.  He has one arm supporting my waist and his other arm steering my left leg toward a leather loop dangling from the ceiling.  He slots in my ankle before seizing my other leg, yanking it as far as it will stretch, then securing my other ankle in another loop.  Hell, my hands can almost reach the floor and my ass can feel air invading.  I'm not too far off doing the splits and it is apparent what this guy likes doing to his ladies.  It's oral sex, sex with his fingers which are about the same width as his shoulders.  And it goes on forever like he's pacing himself and knows precisely how long he can last.  The worse things are his silence and his robotic rhythm.  I prefer movement that varies; slow, moderate, then bang-bang, or slow to bang-bang, or even all bang-bang, but this guy will never get a girl's blood boiling in a month of Sundays.  For the final ten minutes or so he chews on my pussy, but he requires education. And as he finishes, I nearly laugh when he says in a monotone voice, 'That is it for another week.'  I don't expect a tip but receive a twenty-pound note somewhat grudgingly.  I have to ask him to release me; he'd have left me dangling.

I shower quickly because I think it's early enough to get a third client, and very quickly I'm down to the first reserve and hoping for a good warm-up before my encounter with Sally tomorrow.  One of the girls behind me is told by a maid that her driver is waiting.  The buzzer sounds, and off I go to cage 6.

Only ten minutes pass before I hear two exceedingly deep voices asking a maid if I'm a fresh body – they don't recall seeing me.  Am I fit?  The maid mentions my name.  'Give me the key,' says one of the voices.

I'm lifted down by two huge hands, led along the corridor with a different big hand flat on my back, and steered into an unfamiliar room.  The guys agree that they don't want the manacles, then one takes the blindfold off my head and has a good feel of my body like he's testing its firmness.  I see two tall West Indian guys in shorts and t-shirts; they joke with me as if they think I've never had sex.  'How do you like it?' one asks.

'It's how you like it that counts,' I say.  Then I glance around the room; it's sparsely furnished – a few cushioned seats and a whole lot of floor space.

They begin tossing me about, playing a game of catch and in between removing items of clothing.  When their dicks start getting harder, I wonder when they're going to stop swelling.  They notice me staring and ask if I'll have a problem.  I say, 'Try me,' and then the sex begins.  One carries me and walks, the other chases him.  It's, I've got her, I'm screwing her – 'Use the other entrance, man.'

And when they finally consent to stop moving, I'm being held aloft in the middle of the room being doubly penetrated and bounced up and down like a yoyo.  I let myself go, and probably this is the first time here that I concentrate on receiving pleasure.  I tell them with smiles and silly grins that they can do what they want with me – I won't complain; I'm the survivor of a gang-bang and I wear a medal of honor.  I'm back to front, front to back, held vertically, horizontally, with my legs around the smaller guy's

head.  They're happy guys, powerful guys, and they know what to
do with a girl like me.  I get hornier and they respond.  I get
hornier still and they step up a gear, and eventually, they put me
on one of those cushioned seats and finish me off.  They stand
over me laughing, saying I'm a 'good fuck'.  They tease me by
adding they may start again.  Instead, they dress, spread three
fifty pound notes over my belly and press a finger into my nipples.
'We'll take you to a different room next time.  You're getting it
wicked, girl,' says the taller one.

 'You are nice guys,' I say as they leave.

 My biggest tip to date.  My biggest dicks to date.  I'm
happier than hours earlier and I look forward to another day.


**Before the knock on the door**


When Tracey first touched me on the lane that runs behind the
church, she hooked me for good.  No girl had touched me before.
Then when I went to her house and she showed me what
sensations could stir in a body that had been relatively sheltered
from experiments, and she thoroughly abused me until I melted
on her dirty pink bedsheet, I knew my life was changed forever.
There could be no return to a simple girl.

 I intend to do to Sally what Tracey did to me – hook her
forever, but there is a difference.

 Tracey and I exceeded our brief and we ventured on to
the Golf Club.  Although Tracey fell in love with me, she was
always devoted to sex, sex with anyone, sex with any number, sex
for the sake of having sex.  The big difference with Tracey and
Sally is that Tracey was never mine and mine alone; I was her

conquest and her pupil – she didn't ask me to be loyal and nor did she pretend that she'd be loyal to me.

Sally is a child by comparison; she doesn't seem the type of girl who'll suddenly run off to have dozens of affairs.  I give her thrills.  I've never once suggested her outlook should be broader or that she should seek sex when and wherever it is available.  Sure, both Tracey and I were willing to give our bodies to anyone, but with Sally, I want her all to myself.  Harry is entitled to a part of her, but he is incapable of providing that which she needs and that which I have allowed her to taste.

The only two folks who know of our meetings are me and her, and that's how it's going to remain.  She's mine.  I'm going to make her mine.  For her, today will be unforgettable.


**Unrelenting – Paradise Regained**

I improvise, conceal my weapons beneath the bed; alarming Sally is the last thing I wish to do.  She texted me from a position of trust; she reached out bravely in her innocence.  It will be nice to spend time with her.

When Sally arrives, she is dressed in a pale brown dress with matching wet-look brown shoes.  She looks so virginal, like an innocent calling for a Bible lesson.  For the first time, I notice puppy-fat on her face and tell her she is stunning.  'I've missed you,' I say with a single tender stroke of my fingers on her cheek.

'You didn't mind…?'

'Of course not.  I've dreamed of you.'

I make her a coffee and as we're standing in the kitchen, I spin a story of how we have so much in common.  We have partners who don't understand our needs.  I tell her how I left

Marty almost a year ago, how I remained in exile on the South Coast, how I felt empty inside and yearned to find intimacy with someone who also felt neglected.  We can live with another, but often the choices we make prove imperfect.  Relationships always lack something.  What Sally and I have shared is rare and worth holding on to.

I tell her that moving into her caravan was a turning point. When I saw her beauty, when I understood that she seemed just like me, yearning inside for a little more than she presently possesses, I knew I had to get to know her.

Sally kept nodding, and by the time we were sitting close on the sofa, she felt extremely comfortable and didn't regret her decision to come here.  'I never thought that girls could do that,' she said.

'Have sex?'

'Yes.  I can't get those feelings out of my mind – you know... when you touched me.  When we...'

'Connected?' I say.  I place my hand gently on her leg.  She smiles ever so faintly and turns to face me.

Oh God, this is beautiful.  It is beautiful knowing that there is no rush.  Hours lie in front of us and the only obstacle will be a lack of patience.  I peck her lips, and she remains in the same position as if she wants me to keep pecking her, wants to remember how it felt in the beginning when I touched her in her doorway.  Did I touch her or entice her by lowering my knickers?  I don't remember the details.

We sip our coffee.  I say her body is wonderful.  When I look at her, I melt.  Can she imagine the feelings that run through me?  Does she know how my belly churns?

'Me too,' she whispers.

I run my fingers up the back of her neck and she tilts her head, exposing the flesh beneath her chin.  I half kiss her, half lick her until she purrs and closes her eyes.  'How do you do this to me?'

'Because you are magical,' I say.

I do not cease until her body is trembling and I feel her nipples erect beneath the material of her dress.  I ask her how many orgasms she'd like.  She simply shudders.  I say in a low deep voice that soon we are going upstairs to my bed.  I'll undress you.  I'll lay you down and oh so slowly I shall make love to you, and after I make love to you, I'll screw you again and again.  You shall feel sensations that you didn't know were possible.  You'll reach climax after climax as I invest my body in your pleasure. You will come to know how sex can be between us.  I want you.  I am taking you to paradise.

Sally's eyes are submissive as though dulled by thoughts of orgasm; they don't erupt but transmit a dull erotic glow like a photograph of a vagina.  She waits for my lead; she waits on a breath as frail as her resistance and parts her lips to release hope.

'You are the magician,' she says.

'Are you ready?'

She nods faintly, offers me her hand.  We stand like a couple about to be betrothed and proceed gracefully to the stairway in the hall.  Her lovely ass glides over each fertile step.  I touch her hips and I sense her expectations.  And as she sees my bed through the doorway, she glances for permission to enter. 'At last.'  She walks in, I turn her to face me.  'I waited for you.  All those lonely nights wanting you.  You are here.  I adore you, Sally.'

'You are kind to me,' she mumbles.  'So very kind.'

My impulse is to lift her dress, lose myself in her flesh.  I have to battle impatience and restrain my urges.  I touch her

cheeks and then caress her neck.  As cautiously as handling a bird
with a broken wing, I ease her face to mine.  We kiss gently, kiss
and fill the space between our bodies.  Our mouths open and our
tongues meet for the first time; the delicacy, the intimacy of this
moment is sublime.  Her tongue is pure, as soft and sweet as her
lips and it tangles with mine as dancers grooving to love songs.
We are hungry, but time does not rush us; our breasts are heaving
and our hips apply fractions of pressure.  We make love with our
mouths.  We take air, resume, lips to lips, tongue to tongue, teeth
nipping our lower lips and our bodies steadily imparting heat.  Oh,
never have I stood so long in one embrace.  We are virgin lovers
hanging by threads to our virginity.  The thought of rushing
becomes anathema; I desire the petals of every second, the
fragrance and textured inflections of minute tremors and the
rising excitement from within her body.  I desire her
unequivocally.

  We float closer to the bedside; the palms of Sally's hands
steer toward me.  Oh, in this seemingly insignificant action is
expressed a yearning for more.  She rests her tongue on her lower
lip.  She takes a tiny step away from me and her eyes dip.  She
wants me to see her.  She offers herself for sacrifice in an
irresistible pose.  'Take me,' she mouths almost inaudibly.

  My fingers are unsteady as I feel the hem of her dress and
place my face flat to her belly.  She is trembling and juices are
squealing inside her.  And as I slide to her breasts when raising the
dress to her waist, she sighs and I feel her warm breath on my
hair.  Her jaw trembles too and I watch her suck in air as the dress
sails over her breasts and then masks her face ever so briefly.  She
wears pale yellow underwear with ornamental bows.  Slender
knickers, cups of her bra curve downward, and she is sexiness
personified.  I'm so aroused, so very desperate to taste her but

the sight of her partially dressed body is a memory to fix in the mind and keep forever.  'You are beautiful,' I say.  She smiles gratefully.  I see her feet move a whisper and can no longer resist touching her.

I reach behind to unclip her bra and she stirs her shoulders to let me take it from her body.  I do not remember her standing before me while I absorb the fabulous shape of her tits – she's been laid down, reclined in one way or another.  Her tits hang like perfect fruits on a sturdy branch; small pink nipples so delicious to suck; her tits are separate, without cleavage and undeniably youthful.  Oh God, how am I so patient?  How could anyone alive resist such a gorgeous creature?  I treasure the seconds, record the paleness of her skin as I dip to take down her knickers and kiss her several times around her navel.  Her hands move, fleetingly stroke my hair as if she too is refusing to rush, as if she too is turning the tap of sensation by infinitesimal segments. We are screwing already; we are making love in minds racked with desire and our mouths are eating each other from an exquisite distance.

I summon Sally with my eyes to strip me.  I do not invite her: this is a stern demand that she must experience the joys of exposing a body that will ravish her body; she must unwrap the flesh that I shall force her to feed upon although force shall not be used because she will know she is powerless not to taste that which I've stolen from her.  I summon her; do it, step forward reveal me as I revealed you.  My palms face her submissively.  I am yours and I mouth her words, 'Take me.'

This is more than fantastical, more erotic than dreams can manifest.  As she undresses me, I marvel that I do not touch her. Thrills so rare surge in my throat; they crash in my belly and explode like fireworks in my pussy.  I can't recall such vibrations;

to be so aroused at this stage of sex is incredible, and as Sally copies how I undressed her and her lips circle on my belly and my knickers pass down my thighs oh God, I'm dying in a thrill that's rich with eroticism.  This is Sally, the virginal girl I screwed in the caravan most likely against her wishes.  She is taking me where other sexual partners have never ventured.  Her lips fall on my pussy and my resistance snaps like a rubber band.  I moan, my fingernails scrape through Sally's hair and I press her face against me.  My legs rock – I must have her, have her now.

This isn't how it was supposed to be; I planned to devour Sally completely, I thought I must embroil her in a plethora of orgasms before she lost herself and became unable to refuse me compensation.  I'd have her, then she'd satisfy me, and then we'd share what remained of our bodies.  I seize her like I used to seize Tracey after I'd pleased her.  I fall on the bed holding her close. She is above me; I rain rough kisses on her open mouth; our hunger explodes almost instantly and I revolve her body until we are doing what all lesbian girls do better than any man.  There is no intermediate action.  She is as thirsty as me for the luscious taste of pleasure.  We gorge, we gobble, we are gentle and splendidly violet, we use our fingers and our tongues and our faces and feast on the table of each other's delicious flesh. Through an hour, through barriers of past experiences to new fertile meadows.  Through sensations unique, through climaxes that cry and orgasms that are reoccurring.  We escape the world as astronauts; we bathe in utopian pools and drink life's elixir until we are gasping and struggling to breathe.  We are wettened, reddened and stained with fulfillment but when our faces eventually come together, I tell Sally that we have just begun.  She grins in amazement, asks if this is real sex.  I roll her over, then get out of bed and set to work with Marty's fluffy pink straps – wrist to ankle, wrist to ankle.  I lay Sally on her back and drool over her bound and helpless body.  She utters, 'Oh no.'

Again, I crawl off the mattress and show her one by one my selection of implements as I toss them between her legs.  I ask if she'd like to be blindfolded, even gagged.  She contemplates then nods.  And when she is blind and silent, I sit at her feet and adore what lays in front of me.  I spend five minutes telling her what's going to happen next.  I tease her by given her samples.  I tease her until her wriggling body is begging for me to abuse her.  Oh, if I could remain here forever, I think I'd approve.

What I did to Sally, and then what Sally did to me, and later we did simultaneously to each other, has no place to be stored other than in our memory.  I've had sex with Tracey that has been brutal, brilliant and exhausting.  The gang-bang proved incomparable in many ways.  But as for the most beautiful sex of my short life, I can say without a doubt that the four hours I spent with Sally in my bedroom takes the prize.  She went home in a taxi at half-past three in the afternoon.  When Marty arrived at some time after five and he asked how my day had gone I told him unashamedly, 'I've spent all day screwing a girl in our bed.  I'm sorry that the house stinks, but for me, it was worth it.'

'Do I know her,' he said.

'It wasn't Katy or Tracey Cummings.'

'Oh,' he said, 'what's for dinner?'


**A return to confusion**


When Marty goes to the shop at about nine o'clock which is in truth, a swift visit to Katy's kitchen for a quick shag on her table, sofa, or chair, and he'll return to tell me he got chatting to a neighbor, I start pondering how I presently feel.  Answer: ugh!  Answer: not too bad.  Answer: how the fuck am I supposed to know how I feel, and what's that mean?

Financially I'm supported by Marty, my savings are growing, and I have a wage to look forward to that's going to be more than my accumulated tips.  Money isn't a problem.  I even gave Sally a tenner for her taxi.  She may have left the taxi seat stained and in need of a clean.

Sex… now don't ask me to put potential sex partners in order.  I'll say that I definitely want Sally again.  I hope my sister Katy doesn't become devoted to Marty.  I guess I'll always let Marty have a nibble as long as he's not demanding.  The brothers Kev and Timmy are there if I need them.  Geoff if I get super-duper desperate to be touched.  There's elusive Harry who I wouldn't say no to if I bumped into him on a dark night.  And of course, every client that chooses me when I'm spotlighted in one of the cages.  And then there is Tracey Cummings.

Males versus females?  They are different… females, I guess, young females.

Rosa Saint John – who do you love?  If this question were a horse race, I'd say that Katy and Tracey are in the lead with the plodder Marty behind them on the rails.  Coming up fast from the tail is that stunning filly Sally who is lengthening her stride and looks sure to be involved in the finish.

Prediction for the coming week, the coming months… I fear losing at least one of my lovers, and honestly, I don't want to lose any of them.  Indeed, I still hope to find Tracey, and…

## Lost for a while

I'm disinclined to record a thought; each thought conflicts with another.  I wake up happy then I sink into sadness.  One minute I'm proud of being a whore and the next I'm disgusted with myself.  I think I love someone then I think I love another.  I argue with myself then decide there's no reason to argue.

It seems like an age ago that I said this record would be a partial absolution from those who caused me to seek exile.  What I didn't know then but I know now, is that this is a partial absolution of me.  I need to forgive myself for lots of things.  Some days it's easy and some days I feel my crimes are so many and so unforgivable that in another month or two I'll be running off again – to the South Coast, to the South of France, to the South Pole.  Just as before, no-one will miss me.  My parents don't care, Marty will settle down with Katy, Sally will teach Harry what sex is, and SMA will soon find another tart for an empty cage.

Maybe I'll be back in a day or two with lots to say.  Maybe I'll vanish off the face of the earth and be forever elusive... just like Tracey Cummings.


## A fortnight down the line

Am I back on track?  Yes and no.  I often think about those uncomplicated days in the café when I had my eyes on Josivini.  Getting a glimpse of her breasts as she leaned on the counter was a joy, stealing a kiss even better.  Ha, I recall all those fantasies about sharing her bed, they were innocent and wonderful and came to nothing.

And now, closing in on one year later, I have sex at least half the days of my life (more) and the fantasies have withered. I don't appear to be happier but stuck in a routine of mild depression, gathering sensations ranging from five-star to one-star, experiencing the wanted and non-wanted, and contriving circumstances for kicks.

Take the last one... Ten or so days ago I fastened Marty's fluffy pink straps to the legs of our kitchen table after persuading him to invite Katy to dinner because her kids had been dropped off at our parents. It was pure devilment. I just wanted to see how far I could push them, to test if they'd explode and start calling me a perverted whore. When Katy got here, I said dinner will be served if I can watch Marty tie her to the table and drill her ass until she's screaming. They thought I was joking. I really wasn't joking, and in the end, they submitted and I stood at the side of the table with a sulky face with my arms folded and eventually listened to her screams. Am I a sicko? These are two of the folks I'm supposed to love.

It gets worse than that.

The first thing one morning I called at Geoff's to see if his sons were home. They were home, and I got my third helping of a double-up from Kev and Timmy. As usual, I had to walk home across the field without knickers and with semen running down my legs. I blamed Tracey Cummings because she led me to those guys and they were my first betrayal of Marty with males.

It gets worse.

Four times in the past two weeks I've had sex with Sally. The first time was nuts. I'd called at my parents and I'd got them to speak civilly. During gossiping about their new cleaner, I suddenly had an urge to taste Sally's body. I texted her from the side of father's chair and put 'Meet you at the park gates in twenty minutes'.  Yes, I rushed off, met her at the park gates then took her behind the folly on the hill in the park and had her for breakfast.

Another day I took her to the rooftop of the tower block. Another day I brought her to my house and had her on the sofa and the mat in front of the fireplace.  And perhaps the best of the four occasions was by the riverbank because not only did I lose myself in her fabulous flesh she lost herself too in mine.  That girl is so appetizing I don't think I'll ever be able to give her up.

What else has happened?

One afternoon I got chatting to Belinda not too far from the bus shelter on the road that leads from the council estate, then along the bottom edge of the field, before going off toward town.  My eyes nearly popped from my head when I saw what I believed to be one of the Volvos owned by SMA.  I couldn't tell who was in the car but I quickly made an excuse to leave Belinda and go straight to Tracey Cummings' house.  Of course, no-one was there, but the Volvo/Tracy link had me thinking that she too could be working for the Association.

I guess with all this sex I'm giving the impression that I wasn't getting much action on my three nights a week in the cages.  Well, that's a wrong impression – the six shifts that have gone have yielded eighteen single or groups of clients.  I've learned that the poses and outfits in the cage change from week to week, and when I wore my see-throughs on week two I was the most popular girl on display.  I got screwed disgustingly by four guys in their fifties and had the return of the Japanese guys who again put me in the harness hanging from the ceiling.  I've learned that single clients often tip meaner than multiple clients, and more often than not the single clients seem shady and in some secret way desire to harm me which is much different from

wanting to thoroughly abuse me.  It's only about one time out of
three that I get horny, and about one time in every six that I let
myself go.  I've stopped sticking to the rules of how to pose in the
cage; there are little tricks that lure clients and I'm learning fast.
It seems the girls are competitive – who gets the most clients and
who earns the most money has the bragging rights, and as far as I
can judge I and the ginger girl (Lucy) are out in front.

One other thing... three weeks working there and apart
from the clients, the girls and drivers, the only other folks that I've
seen are the maids.  I'm realizing that this doesn't make sense.  As
far as I know, there is no senior girl, no senior driver, and none of
the maids could be described as seniors; they're little more than
kids earning pocket money and every one of them appears the
same age or younger than Sally.  So... who is in charge?  Does
Sonny Mabon or Angela lurk somewhere in the building watching
what's going on through spy cameras hidden in roof lights?  I
don't know, but no business ever functions without a boss.  I've
questioned the girls but I don't get any answers and most of them
are dumb and don't understand why there's a need to know – we
screw for money not to learn the order of command in the good
ship HMS SMA.

Oh, in case folks think I've abandoned Marty, he's been
allowed a nibble or two but he's pretty forgettable without my
input, and recently, I reserve my input mostly for Sally.  He still
has no idea about my job, and neither does Katy or Sally.


## A lesson from nature

It's odd how we observe life, we see the same things day after day
and scarcely take notice.  I saw a pair of hedgehogs roaming in my

rear garden, naturally, I thought of Caroline (Marty's first lover) because she had a bush that reminded me of a hedgehog. Anyhow, I watched the hedgehogs for several minutes late one evening. The next morning, on my way to Katy's for a coffee, outside my house in the middle of the road was a squashed hedgehog. That's how life ends for those of us who don't see what's coming. If we see what's coming, we can be prepared for an outcome.

I talked with Katy. We were sisterly, loving, exchanged one or two kisses that I guess were measuring warmth. She perhaps had ideas that Marty would come between us, that I'd be possessive or tell her to back off. Oh, I love Katy now more than at any time in my past – if she's happy being screwed by Marty, I don't give a damn.

We speak about him in metaphors but we know what each other means. And I also tell her that I've spoken civilly to our parents. She's surprised; it's about time the family is reunited. One of her girls who is off school with the sniffles calls me Aunty Rosa for the first time in a long time. And when I leave, Katy looks happy. She tells me that one of these days she and I will have to do something together, whatever that means and whenever I've got time.


**Wednesday morning at nine o'clock as the day begins**

I've sent Marty off to work with a kiss; that's not unusual, it's extraordinary. He thinks I'm creeping for a favor. He's wrong, maybe it's just my way of tormenting him. I watch him drive off in his car then go to the kitchen to pour myself a glass of orange juice.  My phone pings with a text message and I wonder if it's Sally aching for a lick or two.

The text reads, 'Driver dispatched.  Please be at your designated pick-up point at 10 am.  If inconvenient, please respond.'

I'm puzzled.  Have I been a naughty girl?  Have clients complained because sometimes I lead them further than they have intended to go?  Are other girls saying it's unfair because I'm working for pleasure and not just money?

Ideas keep on coming and I shrug them off; if I get dismissed, surely SMA is not entitled to withhold my earnings.

Madly I think I'll be able to screw Sally seven days a week – at least five if I leave two days for Harry.  And as I get dressed in my see-throughs just to show them what they'll miss out on, I'm making plans to take Sally back to the riverbank.  Que sera sera!

I'm picked up at the local shop soon after ten.  As ever, the driver can't speak and I sit on the rear seat feeling sexy and hot.  No knickers, no bra, high heels, and a whole lot of thigh on display.  A monk would screw me, a fucking polar bear would screw me and by over-using my perfume I smell 100% whore.

The Volvo is met by one of the maids who greets me politely with a girly smile and a courteous nod.  She tells me that Angela is waiting in her office on the ground floor and I think my summoning must be serious but at least I've got to know who runs the place.  'I've not set foot on the ground floor,' I say and the maid reassures me she'll guide me.

I follow the maid, gaze at her super little ass as she enters the building then she turns left onto a long corridor.  I feel like asking for the maid's number and fantasize about her and Sally naked in my double bed.  I get bold, tell her I'd like to see more of her.  She gives me a coy look before tapping on a door.  A few seconds later the door opens and there stands Angela with a beaming smile, 'Rosa… come in, girl… take a seat… how are you?'

I must look worried. 'Okay,' I say.

'It's just an appraisal… we like to tell our girls how they are fitting in.'

'Oh,' I say.

She takes from a drawer those naked photographs from when I visited the office block in the city. She spreads them in front of me and hell, I can't believe how fabulous I look – I've never seen my ass from that angle – no wonder some clients go wild! I'm shocked by how firm my tits look, and God, my hips almost turn me on. I stop looking before I book an appointment to screw myself.

'Very stunning,' she says. 'Your progress report is also stunning. Clients are pleased with you. You are a credit to the business.'

'Thanks,' I say.

'And how do you feel about your work?'

'It's great,' I say. 'Varied…'

'No problems?'

'No.'

'Getting along with the maids and the other girls?'

'Yes. They are lovely.'

Angela leans back in her seat, glances briefly through her window. 'Would you like to earn a bonus?'

I shrug my shoulders, think about asking a question but resist. 'Sure.'

She stands, grins with a hint of amusement in her eyes. 'Let me take you to the Recruitment Manager's office.'

**Emotionally wrecked and physically racked**

Angela pops her head through the doorway of the next office.  I can hear her speaking in a very quiet tone but can't make out what she's saying.  Her hair bobs against the door frame; she's gesticulating with one hand.  Eventually, she steps back, shows me the palm of her hand for me to step into the Recruitment Manager's office.  'You need no introduction,' she says, then off she goes.

I step forward and almost collapse in the doorway.

'Well, Rosa Saint John...'

Tears start pouring down my cheeks as I manage to say, 'Tracey Cummings.'

We stare at each other for about ten seconds before running to each other's arms and start kissing madly, squeezing madly and hugging like we're about to have sex on her capacious desk.  We both speak at once.  'You've pink hair.  It's short.  You look gorgeous.  Oh God, I can't believe it's you!'

'You've still got the see-throughs.  You look a million dollars.  I knew you were here.  I knew I'd see you.'

We hold each other's shoulders and stare eye to eye.  We're both crying, both wishing we'd never parted and both remembering what it feels like in familiar arms.

I tell her I've called at her house a hundred times.  She tells me I've sent her a million texts.  I say I went to the Golf Club and asked for a rerun of the gang-bang.  She laughs, so did she.  I was sent to Sonny Mabon; so was she.  I came back from the South Coast on my birthday.  She knows.  Why didn't she reply to me?  She's still in pain – she hates me because she's still in love with me.  'I hate you too,' I say.  We laugh again, squeeze the last breath from each other's bodies, stroke each other's hair but

Tracey hasn't much hair to stroke.  I kiss her like I've not kissed anyone (maybe Sally apart) in the last year.  We inspect each other's bodies perhaps 69 times.  'The see-throughs,' she keeps repeating.  'The pink hair,' I keep repeating.  I'm deliriously happy and just want to run upstairs with Tracey Cummings and screw her in one of those luxurious beds.

Then Tracey glances at her wall-clock and says she needs to ask me a favor.  She tells me briefly how she first worked the cages then had an accident by falling from a harness.  She was put in charge of room ideas, girl recruitment, the maids, and then client recruitment.  She gets paid a fortune.  She's expecting a few potential members and she needs to sign them up and then give them a tour of the upstairs.  Will I assist her upstairs?  Would I demonstrate how a girl is chosen and maybe explain what can be done in the numerous rooms?  'You're dressed for the part,' she says.

We see a coach pull up outside.  Tracey flaps a little, tells me that if I want to look doubly presentable go grab a shower because she's smudged my lipstick and made me look like a whore who's just had sex in an alley.  I ask her if there's an alley close by.  She flicks out her hand and starts cleaning her face with a tissue.  'I'm going,' I say and then I head toward the staircase and see the maid.  The maid asks me if I already know Miss Cummings.

'Only physically,' I joke, and yes, that maid sure has a lovely ass.

I go to the shower room and spruce myself up.  That's not all I feel like doing but maybe I can catch up with Tracey when the potential clients have gone.  When I'm dry and make-up has been reapplied, I go and sit in the preparatory room with the door open.  I keep glancing at my body in the mirror and find it hard to believe that it's the same body as I saw in the photographs in Angela's office.  That same maid asks me if I'm okay.  I dare to ask her if she's a virgin and she proudly tells me she is.  As she disappears, I shout, 'Things can change,' but off she goes in her black and white uniform probably blushing and preparing a fantasy for when she's alone in bed tonight.

The best part of an hour passes before I hear lots of footsteps on the stairway.  I go to the doorway and see Tracey leading about sixteen or seventeen men aged from mid-twenties to the late forties toward the corridor where the cages are located.  She stops to introduce me, tells the men that I'm one of their star girls.  She winks, then we all pause in a line in front of the cages.  She switches on the spotlights, explains how the girls are selected, and adds that it is customary to tip a girl after a rendezvous.  The girls rely on the tips and they are not finicky about where the tips are placed – that's Tracey's little joke.  She gets me to demonstrate how girls pose and I must say that my see-throughs get a lot of attention.  I hear two of the men say, 'I'm having her for sure.'

Tracey keeps winking at me and I think she's saying I'm being a perfect hostess.  Then from the cages, she takes the men to the rooms.  At each room, she gets me to point out the features and to tell the clients which rooms are my favorites, which are best for individuals and those likely to be preferred by groups.  Tracey adds her comments and the men hang on her every word.  Things are going splendidly and I'm guessing that the tour is not far from being complete.  Then Tracey brushes past me and whispers, 'Got a treat for you, girl.'  We've visited all the rooms I know of and I think she's about to lead us to another staircase at the far end of the building.

She arrives at a double door, says mysteriously, 'Anyone for refreshments?'

Of course, the guys are happy and they tell her in no uncertain terms that they're in no rush.  She opens both doors; there are bars, seats, and tables.  On the main bar are maybe twenty bottles of spirits and about six trays containing glasses.  Tracey invites the guys to enter the room and points to the drinks.  'Help yourselves,' she says.  She winks again, grins cheekily at me.  Then as the men are pouring themselves drinks, she takes my hand and leads me to a table in the center of the room.  She lifts my hand high as if she wants me to stand on a chair at the side of the table.  She nods to encourage me.  I stand on the chair then immediately she raises her hand higher, way above her head.  'On the table,' I mouth.  She nods again.

So, there I am in the center of the barroom with lots of eyes turning to glare at me.  Tracey glances up at me, then suddenly runs her fingers up the back of my leg.  I shoot down an inquiring look.  Tracey turns to the guys and sharply claps her hands to gain their attention.  'Strip off,' she yells joyously, 'Rosa is all yours... don't let her down.  I'll be back in an hour.'  And then she scampers to the doorway and closes the double doors behind her.


**Working overtime**

This is going to be a unique experience, and don't go bringing up the Golf Club last year because then Tracey Cummings was spread-eagled on the next table.  I'm alone, defenseless, and about to be violated in no uncertain terms.  And guess what's my first thought – 10 guesses: one minute to respond.

Answer: I think there's no way I'm going to allow them to damage my see-throughs and immediately start swinging my hips to signal that I'm going to reward them with a sexy striptease.  I notice two of the guys have taken off their shirts and one has already got his pants undone.  I and Tracey always craved another gang-bang but we never spoke of doing it on our own or believed it would ever happen.  Here goes... let's earn the bonus!

I keep giving them a glance at my tits, lift my top side to side, up and down, licking my lips and opening my mouth to show them that it's another entry point.  I'm scarcely a minute in and my body is glowing as I watch the men shift their balance from one foot to the other.  And just as at the Golf Club, the chanting and the clapping begin.  It's plain to see that none expected this initiation ceremony, and neither did I.  I'm shaking inside and feeling an enormous sense of power because I know I can keep them waiting for as long as I like.

When my top comes off all of them move forward, and by the time I start teasing them with my skirt the table is surrounded and hands are reaching out to touch me.  Pants are dropping, the surrounding area is being cleared, and the cries of who's going to have me first are numerous.  My skirt is being tugged and I decide to let it go and yell to the man who has hold of the hem not to damage it.  He throws it over his head and I'm hauled down to the tabletop and co-operating with requests as soon as my back hits the wooden surface.

As the assault begins, I think how similar it is to the gang-bang at the Golf Club.  I'm stretched like a table-cloth; my hair and head are dragged in the direction of erect dicks; I'm shunted up and down the table, penetrated, fingered and every part of my body is mauled.  They're like vultures on a carcass, becoming increasingly daring from one second to the next.  And just as

before, a man climbs beneath me and screws me from behind as
another guy screws me from the front.  There are dicks to the left,
dicks to the right, and more dicks at my face.  I can tell that
they're novices because they lack patience and fear they won't
get a turn.

I surprise myself for being cool, but I think of Tracey's
words... she'll be back in an hour – I need to pace myself and
satisfy the few before I satisfy the many.  And they cum inside me,
in my mouth, on my belly, and my tits.  And I know what is next;
they position me doggy-style and I laugh within and start thinking
that all men are the same but at least my juices will soon be
flowing.  They are in and out, eager to be next, and not choosy
about which hole to enter.  I pray for them to be rougher and I
have to arouse their spirits by banging my ass against them.  Some
come and go in seconds, some are encouraged to be more brutal,
and just as I'm getting my message across, I'm lifted in mid-air and
supported two guys to each limb and another guy holding my
neck.  I yell out, 'Call this screwing!'

Yes, yes – that gets their dicks stiffening and the pistons at
the ready step up a gear and soon I'm nearly choking and spurting
out joy.  'I want fucking,' I scream as an insult.  And that works
too.  The sex turns riotous and it seems like they're trying to screw
me all at once.  Oh God, I let myself go and add to the stickiness
and the thickening stink of the air.  I scream, I moan
uncontrollably, and holler 'fuck me' 'use me' 'batter me' and
anything else I can think of.  They drag me across to the bar and
rest me tit-high on its edge.  My legs are lifted, then guy after guy,
one minute each, starts hammering into my ass, to see if I'll split
in two, to see if I can take the whole length of his dick, to use me
how a whore should be used as though she's not human, as
though she deserves the full punishment of all mankind.

Keep going, keep going, I'll wear you out.  You'll never conquer Rosa Saint John.  'Is this all you can do?' I shout, and they blast me harder, they send my toes to the north and south poles, get me on a bar stool, get my head curled between my legs on the floor.  They treble-up on me, drench me with cum, back to the table, back to the bar, ones, and twos, and threes and fives but they're falling away and only the strongest keep going.  Somehow, I break free then I pose as if I'm undefeatable.  Legs apart, hands on hips, I invite them to take me from back and front.  Two guys get chairs so they can reach my mouth.  I'm lifted inches from the floor as four guys begin to pound me.  It's mayhem, those still with energy want a piece of me.  I'm pushed here and there, tossed through the air from one small group to the next.  One group wants to finger me, the next wants my ass, the next group grips my hair and forces me to suck their dicks.  I'm pleading for something extra-special so I'll have a massive orgasm.  I'm finishing so many off but no guy has the skill of Tracey Cummings to finish me off.

And when I'm back on the center table and the last guy standing finally ejaculates on my tits, I see an image of Sally sitting on my face.  As the stains of the guys' triumph are rubbed on my flesh, I strangely get the idea that sex with Sally is better than anything.  The image of her dies when I see hands pressing banknotes onto the glue that make babies.  Guys are putting their clothes on, opening their wallets and stuffing notes in my pussy as if it's a letterbox.  They cover most of me in notes, tap my head like owners tap puppy dogs.  'You're terrific', 'You're fabulous,' 'See you next time,' 'Love you, babe.'

I hear Tracey's voice.  She says that she hopes they have had fun, and when they are ready, the maids will escort them to the coach.  They leave in drabs.  And when Tracey wanders over to inspect my body she smiles and says, 'They need washing.'

'Eh?' I groan.

She starts pulling banknotes out of my pussy and placing them on top of the others.  'There must be a grand or more.  You did well.  You always said you'd like another shot.'

'Thanks, girl,' I say.

'Stay home tonight, I'll cover your earnings, and won't forget your bonus.'

'You've mellowed, 'I say.

'You look fabulous,' she says.  'Do you feel fabulous?'

'Yes, since I saw you, I've felt very fabulous.'

Tracey plants a kiss on my silver-coated lips then tells me to shower.  She'll come in the car that takes me home.  'I'll drop you off.  We'll keep in touch, and maybe...'

'Maybe what?'

'Maybe... who knows what maybe means.'


**With my head on the pillows**


Is deflated the correct word to describe a mood after dreams have encountered reality?  I find comfort in the warmth of pillows, bury my face and pull the duvet over my head.  There's a couple of hours before Marty gets home and I'm trying to find myself in the interim.  The Rosa Saint John who got in the Volvo at ten isn't the Rosa Saint John who shuts her eyes to block out the daylight.  Five to ten, and I had dreams of finding Tracey and an ever-lurking fantasy to repeat the experience at the Golf Club. Ask me now if I'm satisfied, bursting with joy and feeling on top of the world... somehow, for some reason I'm not.  Half of me is thinking what in future days is going to excite me.  The other half believes it can never be the same again.  Why?  Why?

It's hard to know why.  It's hard to express why a dull white cloud has settled in my brain and no rays of sunshine are penetrating its uniformity.  The best thought I have is that I've got a night off work; my body is my own, aching a little, but for now, it's mine and I shall not sell it for another pile of sticky banknotes. I rub my cheek on the soft Canadian goose down top pillow and oddly think of Sally's inner thighs.  I think of her scent, think of the shade of her skin then crazily question if this morning's gang-bang compares favorably with an hour or two with Sally.  Different experiences, both realities on my sexual journey from a poking on the lane behind the church to gloating on a maid's petite ass in the hallowed chambers of the SMA building.

I curse Sally for being so lusciously sexy.  I urge her to dress in my mind and allow her cloudy colored thighs to temporarily vanish.  Let me think undisturbed.  Let me invent an excuse other than recently being hammered as to why I'm in my bed and feeling sullen.

As a child, my parents took me and Katy to Blackpool for a day out.  I remember being startled by the bright lights, the clicking and whirring of slot machines, the constant blare of old songs, the roller-coaster rides, candy floss, the expanse of the sea – lots and lots of fantastic sensations step after step and minute after minute.  Do you know what…? The second time my family visited Blackpool it wasn't the same – I'd seen it; fascination became remembrance, second-time-around thrills didn't match first-time around thrills.  They weren't brand new.  I now knew what I was going to feel and knew what I was going to see and hear and smell.

Sixteen or seventeen men weren't much different to 20/30 men and women at the Golf Club.  On my back, doggy-style, over the bar, suspension vertically horizontally, this hole, that hole, orifices all, squirting, stinking, that sense of resistance which I knew must be sustained.  A second gang-bang is like a second trip to Blackpool; good but not as amazing as the first trip.  I never began my journey yearning for anything other than mind-blowing sensations – even when the punters at the Golf Club had a whip-round and Tracey and I received over four hundred quid I didn't care.  I took a hundred quid just to appease Tracey.  But this morning I remember seeing all those stained banknotes stuck to my body and thinking that I'd earned them.  Yes, I thought of the money instead of soaking up the pleasure of being abominated.  After the Golf Club, I'd have volunteered to be a victim every single day, but now I think that gang-bangs are no big deal – give me two hours with Sally instead!

And then there's Tracey Cummings.  How many times have I pined for her, been to her house, texted her, walked the streets of the council estate hoping to see her?  I admit, there have been nights I've cried in my bed believing I'll never see her again.  Well, I have seen her again… what happened?

Yes, it proved to be magical.  She looks adorable; holding her was a fantastic experience.  I'd missed her – that little pixie face melted me; those affectionate touches had my heart racing.  And yes, I felt those old feelings that are surely some kind of love and saw love reflected in Tracey's eyes.  And it was me who Tracey asked to her meeting of clients – she could have asked another girl, that gorgeous ginger Lucy, the ravishing blonde.  She knew I desired to be gang-banged again.  She set it up for me because she loves me.

So why the fuck am I complaining?  Is Rosa Saint John never satisfied?

God's truth is that something is missing in Tracey.  In the old days (a year ago) she'd never countenance sending me into battle alone.  Tracey would lead.  Tracey would never be denied an opportunity for sex.  Tracey was sex in all its guises.  She mentioned an accident – she'd fallen from the harness in the room where those Japanese guys love pleasing me.  She's become an office worker, a manager, a keeper of files and a bunch of sharpened pencils.  And I'm asking myself if Tracey is walking on a different pathway and our future can never be the same as our past.  'Who knows what maybe means,' she said.  When you want something badly enough, maybe is definitely.  She didn't so much tell me when she'd be home in her house on the council estate.  She lacked lust.  She did not indicate that we'll end up in bed before the week is out.

If this sounds like sour grapes because the bar room event didn't exceed expectations, so be it.  Another maybe... maybe I'll count the money when it's washed and then view my morning's work in a different light.


**The word is out**


The last time I called at my parents' house I'd progressed from a classification of sub-human to semi-human; if I hadn't had that urge to get it on with Sally then I may have been promoted to the second daughter by now.

I take a chance, open their door like it's the entrance to a bank vault and squeak meekly, 'It's only me.'

I could have experienced a heart attack when mother shouts, 'Come in, Our Rosa,' and father echoes her words. Don't tell me the cleaner has jacked it in and they're hoping I'll stick the sweeping brush up my ass and do a few laps of the downstairs rooms.

Mother gets up from her chair and points for me to sit on the piano stool. I consider asking if they're sure my bottom half won't contaminate the fabric. Zipped-lips, I sit dutifully (however you sit dutifully!) and smile at father as he folds his newspaper.

He keeps quiet and waits for mother to return from the kitchen with a cup of tea and two chocolate biscuits on a small plate. When she passes them to me, I think I must have fainted and woke in a dream. Mother, making ME a cup of tea! Mother, disposing of two biscuits to the girl who starred in a porn movie! A mountain of suspicion swamps me and the piano stool; there's a wisp of a smile on mother's face – the cleaner must surely be dead.

Her fingers play that tune that Marty plays on our chair arm. She looks at me like I'm her favorite newsreader of the television. 'Well…' she mumbles.

'Well, what?'

'Has Marty been bringing you flowers and chocolates?'

'Eh?'

'You can't fool me, Our Rosa.'

'You've lost me,' I say. 'Fool you about what?'

'My grandchildren come here you know.'

'And…'

'And children talk. Children like to get things off their chest… just like you,' she adds referring to my bra.

'I haven't made another movie if that's what you think,' I say.

'From what I understand,' says mother self-satisfied, 'it's your sister and Marty who've been making movies.  What's he doing at Katy's house when you're not there?  It beggars belief.  And you can't say it's not true, my granddaughters have told me what goes on.'

'So, what goes on?'

'I'm asking you,' says mother.

'They're friends,' I say.

'Your man and sister are friends? – don't be so ridiculous.  What would you think if I let your father go to my sister's house all the time?'

'You haven't got a sister…'

'If I had a sister…'

'Father would be getting a little extra,' I joke.

'Precisely,' snaps mother.  'Don't you think you should keep your man under control?'

'I'm not his keeper.'

'Is Our Katy his keeper?'

'Ask her,' I say.  'I've got my own life to live without worrying about Marty and Katy.'

Mother slaps father on the arm.  'Do you hear that…?  She's not bothered.  Our Katy and Our Rosa are sharing a man, and she's not bothered.'

'Children invent stories,' I say.  I chomp on the biscuits then wash them down with the tea.  Father peeps at me cheekily.  Mother's digits are twitching uncontrollably but if she wants to know more, then she'll have to ask Katy.  I tell them Katy's had a hard time lately, what with Brian going to Scotland and having to take on a job.  I support her how I can.  I love her.  And finally, my mother suggests there is a limit to love and it stops at hiring out a partner's private bits.

'God, that's under the belt,' says father comically.


**WARNING**

Katy answers my call.  'Hi,' I say.  'I thought I'd warn you that mother is not only sniffing the fabric on top of the piano stool where I sit, but she's also asking questions about you and Marty.'

'Really?' says Katy.

'I think she's been talking to your girls.'

'Oh.'

Katy doesn't know what to say.  'I love you, sis,' I say.  'I'm with you whatever happens.  Me and you, forever.'

'Thanks, Rosa.  I love you too.'

'I just thought that you need to be prepared for an inquisition.'


**First thoughts of confession**

Some thoughts we have aren't particularly delineated.  When someone believes or doesn't believe in God the explanation of the reason to believe or not believe is often shady or dubious.  We instinctively respond to questions with 'yes' or 'no' but if we had to dig deep before replying our answers may be different.  I had the thought to gather the folks in my life around the kitchen table and divulge the evidence of who I am – be open, be honest and allow them to judge me knowing the full truth of my circumstance.  I challenge the reason why I keep secrets.  Is it fair to withhold the facts of the real me from the likes of Marty and Katy?  If Tracey Cummings means so much to me (and I am not

clear how much she does mean) then who am I protecting by not
declaring how I feel?  From the moment I got the hots for Josivini,
I've been living a lie.  Confession… who knows, but maybe it is
something to think about.


**Wandering eyes**

By the time I was standing outside the local shop waiting for the
Volvo, I'd almost convinced myself that in the next few weeks I'd
be losing one or two of my lovers.  For some daft reason that has
no foundation whatever, I'd imagined receiving a text from Sally
which declares her love for Harry and unfortunately, she must
give me up because they're trying for a baby.  Potty!  I guess that
is because I fantasize about her more than anyone – fear of losing
her, perhaps?

And because I'd sent Tracey a couple of texts and she
hadn't replied I wondered if she'd gone cold on me too.

And as for Marty and Katy… well, if mother senses
something is happening, then I KNOW that something is
happening.  Deep down, Marty is the type of guy who wants one
woman for himself.  Oh, he had that fling with Caroline, but she
can't hold a candle to Katy.  I feel he's drifted so far toward my
sister that he's not going to find a way back to me, not that I want
him to, but I'd prefer to be something more than friends.

The Volvo pulled up, and I got the mad idea to strengthen
the working friendships I have with one or two of the girls at SMA
– and I knew which ones interested me.

The first greets me as I step from the car; she's that pure
virgin maid who took me to Angela's office.  'You're so cute,' I
whisper in her ear.  As the driver moves the car to a parking bay, I

press my hand on the maid's ass.  She half turns her head and gives me a look that says, 'You're not supposed to do that.'

'You're the most beautiful girl in this building,' I say.  She blushes then lets me walk past her.  Just as I'm mounting the stairs, I look back and mouth, 'I'll have you.'

Then in the preparatory room, as confident as I've ever been, Lucy, the ginger-haired girl who looks like she's stepped from a Rossetti painting, tells me we are reserves two and three.  I laugh, 'We've time to have sex in the shower,' I say.  From her look of surprise, I can tell she's not disinterested.  She stands square on to me, whips off her bra and covers herself ever so slowly in a bathrobe.  I press the advantage, 'I have a thing for gingers.  God, you're sexy.'

She hoists back her neck and says she didn't realize I'd noticed her.  How can anyone fail to notice her?  'Thanks.  Thanks a lot,' she says.

I'd got her attention.

Tonight's outfit is black stockings, a black suspender belt, black cup-less bra, and a black blindfold and scarlet lipstick.  We have to pose with our ankles two feet apart, and when the first six girls are ready, they are led by a maid to the cages.  The buzzer sounds to indicate that a client or clients are on their way.  I'm sitting next to Lucy admiring the contrast of her pale freckled skin against the black when another maid walks into the preparatory room.  She beckons me to the doorway, says in a low voice, 'Special request.  Put on your blindfold.'

I do as I'm told.  She takes my hand and leads me along by the cages.  I can hear footsteps behind us and have no thought as to what's going on.  Then I hear her opening a door; she taps my bottom as though urging me to enter.  I step forward a few paces, the door closes behind me.  Suddenly my blindfold is eased from my head.  'We couldn't resist,' says a guy with a familiar voice.  I see a large double bed, then turn.  There are four guys from Wednesday morning drooling over my body in a semi-circle.  This time they want more than a sixteenth of me.  It will be more fun with just the five of us.

'Hello,' I say.  'You remembered me.'

'How could we ever forget?' says another guy.  And then their fun begins.

From the outset, it appears obvious that the guys have a well-rehearsed plan; they'll take it in turns on this bit or that bit of my body, in ones or twos, in rotation, and they'll take up at least half of my shift screwing me.  They'll spend a certain amount of time warming me, then build the heat and all the while restrain themselves from going crazy – they'll save that for the very end.

They paced themselves, treat me with dignity, ensure that pleasure isn't just theirs.  And boy, as I'm in a mood to receive special treatment the sex proves as good as anything from my previous shifts.  I can tell by the comments and their far-away looks that they are having a ball.

They want me again; they'll join my fan-club.  I'm told I react and don't fake pleasure.  Can they take me home?  Maybe they can screw me twice a day.  They'll rent a flat and keep me as their special plaything.  And hell, I get two hundred quid in sticky banknotes before they leave.  When I return to the preparatory room the girls can't believe I've been screwed for two hours.  There's a big grin on my face and I'm still feeling horny and wonder what's happening to Lucy.

I got one other client who seemed to me like a lady from the legal profession.  She came across as cold and lacking in ideas.  She wanted me to keep on the blindfold after first taking it off my head.  Around forty with a good body for her age, she put me on a

long cushioned recliner sofa with my legs parted over the backrest
and she sat on my face for about thirty minutes and demanded
that I worked on her.  Occasionally, I'd get a poking, but little else.
She spoke briefly.  She moaned quite a bit when she finally
erupted but otherwise, she stayed quiet.

Before she dressed and left, she made an excuse about
not carrying cash and said she'd go to the office and tip me with
her credit card.  What a cow, and she tasted stale!  As if the office
is open at one in the morning!

Before I get called to be taken home, I talk to Lucy for ten
minutes.  She tells me she's had two elderly clients whose
erections were like floppy sausages; they each coughed up a
twenty-pound note.  I hug her, say jokingly that I'd give a fifty for
half her body and she jokes that she'd give me it for free.  As I
leave, I blow her a kiss: it's always good to have reserves.


**Rising to new lows**

There are some events that I have no qualms about recording and
others which I find embarrassing to talk about.  Sure, I'm a whore,
but I'm human too.  It's not nice when folks think bad about me.
It's nice to be liked – being popular is better than being an
outcast.  But the truth is the truth and that is what confessions
are supposed to be.

Here goes…

I get home, of course, Marty is sound asleep, and for an
hour or two I snuggle at his side in our bed and maybe nod off for
a while.  But as the dawn breaks, I'm laid on my back going over
the thoughts I had while waiting for the Volvo about six hours ago.
I calculate that Marty is going to leave me for Katy and I start

fantasizing about Lucy and the pure sweet maid taking their place. Then I get to imagine a life where Sally, Tracey, Lucy, the maid and I are all living in the same house – this house – and how fabulously we could live. How many orgies could be fit in a day even if I kept my job at SMA? Life could be one permanent orgasm. And in my head, I try to visualize how we'd all connect and what, if any, would be the problems.

From this scenario, I go on to speculate that perhaps I'd keep Sally a secret. I've always said that I'd hate sharing her. Then I progress to keeping the maid as secret too. Oh God, if I'm disinclined to share Sally then how could I share such a perfect little virgin?

I'm left with four worlds that are each wonderfully erotic. The group of me, Tracey and Lucy, Sally on the riverbank and the top of the tower block, and cute-assed maid wherever I could have her. Is that perfection or what? And then as I'm getting horny thinking of what could be in the future, I become aware that I'm messing about with Marty even though he's asleep. I deliberate, shall I? I deliberate for about a minute before pushing away the duvet and mess about with Marty a little more seriously. Soon, I'm astride over his body and having sex with him. He's hardly co-operating with me but at some point, he becomes conscious and asks not unreasonably what I'm doing. 'I'm screwing you,' I say. Marty acknowledges my words but doesn't stir more than is necessary. I keep on screwing him like it's the filthiest sex act I've committed in my life. To say he woke up, enjoyed it, or even cooperated a little, is probably a lie. When it's over I must go to sleep because four hours later when I wake, he's gone to work.

**Forlorn – pitifully sad and abandoned or lonely - unlikely to succeed or be fulfilled**

I washed the breakfast dishes as Marty stood in the rear garden gazing at the sky; he always does that on Saturday morning when he's not working.  Today though, I just knew he was thinking of Katy because occasionally he shook his head like he has another problem – and that problem is me.  It's one thing abandoning me to go live with Caroline (a woman I despised) but completely another when he's thinking of running off into my sister's bed.

I felt sorry for him and sorry for myself and suddenly when the water whirled down the plughole I thought of the word 'forlorn'.  I looked it up in the dictionary that stands on a shelf in our room: pitifully sad and abandoned or lonely, and, unlikely to succeed or be fulfilled.

Spot on.  How does a lexicographer find such an accurate description of me?

I need someone who'll listen to me, an ear to fill with moans, someone who'll brush off what I say and won't remember a word of it.  Katy is not working, presumably, but she's too involved.  Tracey remains distant, she hasn't responded to my texts.  Harry is not working, presumably, and he's likely got Sally under observation.  I pick up my phone, madly send Sally a text, 'Call me if you can.'

She phones ten minutes later.  I ask if she'll meet me for a chat, I'm down in the dumps – please wear 75 layers of clothing if you agree – although I desire your body like nothing else on earth I need to unburden my soul and find a smile from somewhere.  Sally says she'll meet me at the burger bar on the main road near the park in half an hour; she can spare half an hour but after that Harry will get suspicious.  My beautiful friend!

We meet.  She's loving and sympathetic.  Over a burger and milkshake, I pour out all my woes that are simple tales of emptiness and rejection.  I feel that I don't belong to anyone.  I tell her about my travels on the South Coast, how I'd watch the sea for hours and purposely bore myself to death, how I'd walk on the beach until I was walking in the footsteps I'd made hours earlier, how sometimes I was so lonely I'd talk to seagulls but the seagulls weren't interested in anything but finding a scrap of food.  I ask Sally if she truly loves Harry.  She says sex with me is better than sex with him – that's no kind of answer.  In some mad way, I hoped she'd say that she'd like to spend her life in my bed not only having sex but drowning me with love.  Sally holds my hands over the table; her hands are like a child's hands and as soft as satin.  She tells me that life is a compromise as though she's got the wisdom of a fifty-year-old.  But time passes quickly and before we know it, half an hour has passed and she has to return to Harry.  We could meet on Monday or Tuesday; we can have sex and she doesn't mind where I take her.  Sally goes home.  I sit at the table for another ten minutes letting tears drip into the banana milkshake.

On my way home I send Tracey yet another message, 'I guess that you don't love me anymore.'  That's it, if she doesn't reply I'm going to put my energies into netting Lucy or the virgin maid with the cute little ass.  I want someone to love and someone to love me for the whore that I am.


**Deluded or doesn't care?**

I record the past day and a half as a non-event.  Marty vanishes twice for two hours at a time to the shops (Katy's) and I've drunk so much orange juice but I don't feel fruity.  As I dress for work Marty almost ignores me.  He doesn't ask questions.  He either still believes I'm frequenting night clubs or he simply doesn't care where I go or what I do.  A few minutes before I leave to meet the Volvo at the local shop he says, 'We're drifting apart, girl.'

'I come home to you,' I say.

He pulls a wry smile.  'Yes, I suppose you do.'


**Last shift of the week before payday**

I promise myself on the way to work that if I see the little delightful maid, she's getting more than a tap on the ass.  I'll proposition her – I'm so desperate I think about suggesting a night in a hotel.  I'll double her wages, I'll be gentle with her, and if she just wants to kiss and cuddle on the first date, hey, that's my treat too.

The Volvo pulls up but no maid is waiting.  I enter through the large doorway and Tracey Cummings greets me with a warm smile.  I'm shocked.  'What are you doing here?' I say.

'Just hanging about,' says Tracey.

'Are you… working the cages?'

'My cage days are over,' she says.

'You haven't answered my texts.'

'Sorry.  It doesn't mean I haven't thought about you.'

I'm thinking on my feet, searching for a way to get her to commit to something.  'You look gorgeous,' I say touching her new pink hair.

'I'm going to go back blonde,' she says.  'And I don't like it short.'

'Doesn't matter how you look to me.'

'That's sweet,' she says.

I blast out without thinking, 'Come for dinner at my house, Monday.' Her expression is difficult to read. 'I'll make it a foursome, Marty and my sister Katy – Marty's got the hots for her. No sex, promise, just a meal, six o'clock. Please...'

She puts her hand on my arm. 'Shouldn't you be heading upstairs?'

'Give me an answer – say 'no' and fucking wound me. Say something.'

'I'll be there,' she says then turns and walks off toward the ground floor corridor. I'm doubtful she means it but as I watch her depart, I notice for the first time that she walks with a slight limp.

I'm then greeted by a maid, but not the maid I was hoping to see. She takes me to the preparatory room where the girls seem to be wilder than usual. Lucy and the blonde girl are at the mirrors already in their outfits. The maid gives us a five-minute warning and when I realize I'm late I have to rush to get ready. I'm in cage 2 and only just make it for the lead out.

As soon as we're in the cages the buzzer sounds. I hear a young very posh voice choose a girl a couple of cages to my left. Within seconds the buzzer sounds again and then another girl is chosen by another young guy with a plum in his mouth. I get picked third and am led quickly to a room. The maid closes the door and immediately the client takes off my blindfold; he's brought me to what we girls call 'The Torture Chamber' but by the look on his face he's chosen the first room available. I guess he's a rich student or even a kid from a private school. He stares at me, then stares at the machinery. He picks up a whip and asks me what it's used for. 'Whipping,' I say. 'Oh,' he says. Then he touches a large dildo and asks what that's used for. I sigh and think he's come to the wrong place.

Then he stands as close as he dares and asks if I keep on the outfit. I tell him it's his choice; he goes bright red everywhere but his chin. I'm embarrassed for him. I encourage him to choose what he wants me to do. 'I like the boots,' he says. 'How old are you?'

'Twenty-six,' I say.

His eyes protrude like the greatest wish of his life is about to be fulfilled. He's probably wanted to screw an older woman since he was in short pants. He forgoes the privilege of torturing me and asks me to lean against the wall. In three minutes maximum, he opens the top front of his pants, takes a while to discover where my entry point is located, has sex with me in the one position, and hands me thirty pounds while expressing his gratitude.

I return on the narrow corridor to shower laughing my head off, and when I get to the preparatory room there is one other girl who is also laughing. These young boys are coming thick and fast and the girls are rotating as fast as they can shower. In minutes, I'm in a cage again, getting screwed again by a small lad who can barely reach me and also chooses the wall as a backdrop. Another thirty pounds. Another return to the preparatory room where I learn that the first batch of clients has been served. It's just gone eleven, or so we believe, and all girls but one, have been shagged twice.

My next odd encounter is with a man and his wife who are out on their wedding anniversary. They are easy to please and simply desire to watch a girl please herself. He's called Jim and she's called Ruth. They've been clients since SMA opened its doors and they love coming here. I put on a show that lasts no more than fifteen minutes and then receive a forty-pound tip and a handshake from both of them.  When I catch up with Lucy, she tells me she's performed for the couple many times; after they've watched her, they go home for a quickie in their four-poster bed.

My final client revolted me when I saw him in the room where girls get tied star-shaped to a spinning wheel.  The guy had a great fat belly, looked untidy and grunted as he moved.  He dished out orders with grunts.  He grunted as he bound my ankles and wrists.  I feared he was going to slaver all over my body or put his mustached mouth where I didn't want it to go.  But hell, that fat guy's looks were deceptive, what he could do with his hands and fingers no matter where I'm at on the wheel leaves no desire wanting.  He blew my mind; he had me oozing and yelling for him to keep going.  I even got flashbacks to Tracey Cummings' bedroom when she first annihilated me with her sex toys.  I won't complain if he chooses me again though he could have been more generous with his tip.

The only other noteworthy mention is that I stole a kiss from Lucy in the shower area.  I told her that her body turns me on.  I've never had a ginger, and I want one like yesterday.  She said she'd think about it.  'Don't take a lifetime,' I said.


**Preparing for the moment of truth**

I sleep in; I guess the fat guy did more for my body than I realized at the time.  I slept like a baby after a full bottle of tinned full-formula milk.  I think about going straight to Katy's to invite her to dinner – who'll mind her daughters? what will she think when I tell her Tracey Cummings is coming, coming to dinner and not to have sex.

I chicken out.  I phone Marty at work.  Dear Marty, my long-time lover and possibly soon to be my brother-in-law or something akin, I've invited a guest to dinner and told the anonymous guest that you'll be there with my wonderful sister whom you've screwed many, many times and hope to screw many more times in the coming weeks.  It will be easy for you to persuade my wonderful sister to take her children to their grandparents before sitting down to dinner around our kitchen table with the anonymous guest.  For once, yes, for once dear Marty, there shall be no sex, not even with the vegetables.  For once dear Marty, grant your long-time partner a favor before you are no longer around to ever, ever use your cable-ties to incapacitate her limbs again.

'Hi, Marty, do you think Katy will come to dinner at our house, about six, leave the kids at our parents – I've invited someone over, I'd like you both to meet her?'

'No problem,' says Marty.  'I'll go to Katy's from work. See you around six.'

'I knew you wouldn't let me down.'


**Contingency plan**

If… that's a big word… IF it all goes wrong I'm going to get an extension to the landing railing, have the landing railing come down the stairs, do a lap of the room and a lap of the kitchen, and then a lap of the garden and maybe out into the street, and then one by one I'm going to lure in turn, Sally, Lucy, the little pure maid, Katy (if I can get her from Marty's grasp), the Japanese guys, the four guys who tipped me two-hundred quid, the fat guy with the busy hands, the brothers, all the other maids, all the girls at

SMA, maybe Harry (I'm not sure), to the railing and use up all Marty's cable-ties and spend all my days having sex with whichever takes my fancy at any particular moment.  If it all goes wrong, I'm going to forget about love and be the dirtiest whore in the history of whoring.  This is my last shot at being a deal-maker. If Marty wants Katy and Tracey wants me, I'll know by seven or eight o'clock.  If not, I'm on the phone to a local joiner – hurry up with the wood, the hammer and nails!


**Bombs away!**


Cooking curry is beyond my area of expertise (what isn't?) but as things may get decidedly hot, I think hot mouths and molten lava leaking from assholes could be appropriate.  It's make or break time.  It's happiness or misery.  Into the Valley of Death rode the two whores, the partner, and my sister.

I dress in a gorgeous red two-piece with moderate heels. It's respectable, makes me look twenty-six instead of nineteen. Make-up light, hair dangling at my shoulders; I'm wearing knickers and a bra so not planning on a celebration foursome.  Marty's pink fluffy straps are safely in a bedroom drawer and the tomato ketchup bottle remains in the kitchen cupboard.  Marty calls at ten to six to say he and Katy are on their way.

Wouldn't I prefer to be dining on Sally at the riverbank?

Wouldn't exploring Lucy's freckles excite me more?

And what about the virgin maid – oh God, am I lost in the City of Debauchery?

The minutes tick by.  Marty and Katy arrive and my nerves are frazzled.

I hand them a glass of wine and oddly we're like strangers at a cocktail party.  We speak politely – nice day, the sun is out, a good day for drying laundry.  How many shags have you had (that is facetious)?  'Has your guest not arrived?' says Katy.

'She'll be here,' I say confidently crossing my legs instead of my fingers.

Marty and Katy are on the sofa and I'm standing by the window when a Volvo draws to a halt on the road.  I go to the doorway; Tracey hurries toward me, 'I'm not late, am I?'

I kiss her, lead her into the house.  Neither Marty nor Katy knows who she is.  Oh, they are aware of a girl with a unique reputation and Katy has seen the film from the Golf Club in which Tracey's face isn't shown.

The happy couple stand, offer their hands politely.  There are 'hellos' 'pleased to meet yous' before I prepare to drop my first nuclear bomb.

'I'm Katy,' says Katy.

'I'm Marty,' says Marty.

I find my hugest smile, 'This is Tracey Cummings, my partner in crime,' I say.

I've got to admit they took it well; they were both still standing and touching Tracey's hands.  Neither had ever touched a whore before other than me.

Then came the small talk, the compliments on outfits, talks of the curry and views on red and white wine.  Tracey came across as an amiable woman, sensible, charming, not speaking out of turn and not asking questions.  I felt like recalling details of the Golf Club gang-bang to rock Marty and Katy from their propriety.

We ate our meal in the kitchen without hiccups, but as we got from our chairs to return to the main room, I noticed two slightly alarming things.  The first is that Tracey seemed to stumble when she took her supporting arm from the back of the seat, and the second is that Marty's face revealed that he was preparing some kind of speech.  Is he going to steal my thunder?

After pouring another glass of wine Marty turns to Tracey and me in the armchairs and begins, 'I'm glad Tracey is here.  This is perhaps best said to both of you.'

'We're a couple,' I joke to Tracey.

Tracey doesn't smile but nods not too convincingly.

'Let's be frank,' says Marty, 'I once quit before and left Rosa in the shit.  She couldn't afford to keep this house going.  In retrospect that wasn't fair.'

'You should have sent money addressed to Rosa, South Coast of England,' I joke.

He pauses for a moment, connects Tracey and me with his eyes like we're a pair of penniless strays.  'What if I pay half of all the bills, mortgage included?'

'So, you're going to Katy's?' I say.

Katy bows her head then reaches out her hand, 'Not if you don't agree,' she says meekly.

Marty searches for a response from Tracey.  Tracey keeps her thoughts to herself.

'I and Katy both have jobs, we're on decent money.  We don't mind supporting you as long as you're happy.  Money isn't everything in life.  I want all of us to be content.'

'And I do too,' adds Katy.

I reiterate the facts.  'You go live with Katy and pay half of the bills for this house,' I say.

'Yes... yes...' says Marty firmly.

'No restrictions... you're not going to dictate conditions or what I do?'

'I never have done,' he pleads.

I turn to Tracey, 'Well, girl?'

'I can't tell you what to do,' says Tracey.

There are lots of stares, lots of weighing up what each of us is thinking. I get the impression that Marty is keen to get out of the front door carrying Katy over his shoulder with her knickers already dangling from her toes. Stupidly, in my head, Tracey is already half-way up the stairs and I'm ripping off her clothes and gasping. I'm dreaming of screwing her until my first shift on Wednesday evening.

'When are you planning on going?' I ask Marty.

Marty and Katy join eyes. The answer is obvious. 'As soon as you like.'

'I love you guys,' I say. 'Let's do it.'

Katy asks if I'm sure. I tell her no matter what happens, I and she have found each other; there's no going back, she's my sister for life. I'll call occasionally to catch her in the shower. Katy laughs, a mild easy laugh that's full of love. She stands preparing to leave. I kiss her, touch her below her navel and tell her to have fun. Marty says he'll return later for some things. I make another joke, 'He won't get you pregnant, he shoots blanks.' They leave. Tracey Cummings is sitting like an orphaned child in a large armchair and she doesn't know what to say.

I kneel before her, run my fingers through her short pink hair. 'Move in with me. Let's catch up on old times.'

'Rosa...'

She doesn't continue but keeps on looking at me as though she's a failure. 'I love you,' I say.

'I love you,' she says, 'but...'

'But what?'

'Since my accident, I'm not the same. You're thinking I'm the Tracey Cummings from last year. You know, wham-bam

Tracey with a different guy for each day of the week; the girl whose magic served a whole generation.'

'Move in,' I say.

'I've two homes already.  I've kept the house on the estate but I spend most of my time in a small flat next to my office.'

'That's why you were there?'

'Sure.'

'Move in.'

'I'll disappoint you, Rosa.  I'm not an athlete anymore.'

'I don't care.'

'You will care in a week or two.'

Tracey won't change her mind.  She calls the Volvo driver who's parked up somewhere close by.  She must go.  She's not willing to ruin my life by denying me sex.  She tells me to screw all the girls at SMA.  As I cry, I tell her about the maid who was with us the other day.  The maid's name is Moira.  Tracey thinks she came from a children's home.  There are a million girls who can give me what I need but Tracey Cummings is unavailable.

I sob and my heart is erupting.  I feel pains in my chest as the Volvo pulls up outside.  Tracey kisses me, tells me to call at her flat.  We can have a coffee.  She leaves and I wave through the window.  I'm crushed, alone, and it hasn't worked out like I hoped it would.


**Middle of the night**


Rosa Saint John can't die.  The clients would complain if I were lifeless.  My heart is already dead.  My sexual desires will be here tomorrow and all the tomorrows that will be.  If this is the end of my relationship with Tracey then I must look forward to other adventures.  Lucy and Moira are waiting in the wings and Sally stands center-stage.

Who knows, Marty and Katy may take pity on me and call for a threesome.  Old Geoff may splash out on a box of little blue pills and claim he can perform miracles.  There has got to be a future, there has got to be renewal.

It's 3.12 am and I text Sally.  'As soon as you can, get here… it's going to be fabulous.'

Rosa Saint John will return; if I can't get love, I'll take pleasure.  Keep on funding me, Marty, you're not cut out to be a step-father.

P.S. An email arrives… my wage slip… pay for four weeks – FIVE-THOUSAND-TWO-HUNDRED-POUNDS including bonuses. Who's crying now?

**The End.**

'      Thank you for reading my novel 'Partial Absolution'. If you enjoyed the story, I'd be very grateful if you left a review on Amazon.  Many thanks, Ken Ross


**Please take a look at my other novels**

www.ingramcontent.com/pod-product-compliance
Lightning Source LLC
Chambersburg PA
CBHW071614150726
48000CB00004B/1717